ALL THE RAVE

TIM LAHAYE
AND BOB DEMOSS

W PUBLISHING GROUP™

www.wpublishinggroup.com

A Division of Thomas Nelson, Inc.
www.ThomasNelson.com

FOR ROBERT AND DORA DEMOSS,
THE MOST WONDERFUL PARENTS ON EARTH.
YOU'RE ALL THE RAVE IN MY BOOK.

———————

ISBN 0-8499-4320-5

Printed in the United States of America
01 02 03 04 05 PHX 9 8 7 6 5 4 3 2 1

THE AUTHORS WOULD LIKE TO EXTEND
THIER APPRECIATION TO:

- Marty Thorson, Kiev, Ukraine, for his Russian translations and insight into the Russian underworld.
- Dr. Shaun L. Reynolds D.V.M., Williamson County Animal Hospital, Franklin, Tennessee, for his invaluable insight into the very real dangers of ketamine.
- The friendly staff of the Brentwood, Tennessee Residence Inn for their exceptional service.
- Leticia DeMoss, Rebecca Wilson, and Nancy Rue, for their editorial input and for being the best grammar police around.

I t was 10:33 P.M. Friday night. A seventeen-year-old girl lay curled in the fetal position on the second level of an abandoned warehouse in downtown Philadelphia. Though her eyes were slammed shut, in her mind she could see herself hovering, phantomlike, above her body.

The dark, rat-infested room where she lay crumpled on the floor spun out of control to the pulsating sounds she could hardly miss, yet couldn't fully hear. A high-pitched frequency, like a carpenter bee looking for a place to drill, whirled in her right ear. She wanted to swat at the source of this annoyance, but her right arm remained unresponsive. Her legs felt numb, and she discovered that they, too, refused to respond when commanded to move.

Her throat was dry—yet somehow was as tacky as flypaper. She tried to swallow but was incapable of that simple task.

Her lungs, attempting to pull in the thick night air through her pierced nose, were greeted by a nasty mix of fumes and dust. She longed for just one full, clean breath of fresh air.

She struggled to fight back the waves of panic. What was happening to her? Why did her guts feel as if they were about to explode? Why was she perspiring when she felt so cold? Why was she wearing pixie wings and pink sneakers?

Just then, her tongue reported something was jammed into her mouth. Her teeth clamped down on its rubbery surface and wouldn't let go. With some effort, she forced her mind to focus. Like the headlight of an approaching car on a foggy night, a dim recognition of the object cut a path through the haze in her head.

A pacifier. How odd.

As she struggled to make sense of the competing sensory input, she was vaguely aware of an acidic bile traveling between her stomach and throat. The bitter, brownish yellow fluid ejected by her liver, like hot lava pushing its way against the surface, battled for immediate release.

More than anything she wanted to vomit.

Then got her wish.

Her mind raced in slow motion, searching for an explanation. Maybe it was a touch of food poisoning.

No. No. NO!

Look what you've done. Face it. You screwed up, big time. What are you on? She was fairly certain the voice echoing inside her head, though familiar-sounding, wasn't her own.

Or was it? It was so difficult to tell.

Was she dead? Was this the last stop before hell? She knew she wasn't ready to die. Certainly hadn't planned to die.

She knew she couldn't speak, yet a feeble voice from someplace inside whispered, *Oh God . . . if you're there, I could use a little help right about now. I . . . Jesus, I . . .*

A sharp pain seared her left arm, interrupting her cry for help. The limb, which had been sandwiched between her body and the hardwood floor, throbbed and demanded to be recognized. She remembered something about a needle, a tranquilizer . . .

With a head full of unanswered questions, she passed out—again.

I'm not changing my mind, Heather. And that's my final answer," Jodi Adams said with a mock Regis accent. Her attempt at humor was met with an extended pause on the other end of the phone. She figured her best friend, Heather Barnes, must really be ticked.

"Why are you being such a stinker? I bet it's because everybody thought Kat's idea was better than yours . . ."

"As if I'm that shallow." Jodi switched the portable phone to her other ear and then glanced at the digital clock on the microwave. Almost 5:00 P.M. She'd been talking for close to an hour.

"I mean," Heather said, "I thought your idea of going to Atlantic City was cool, but I was outvoted. Why can't you just deal with it?"

"Heather, we've already been over this, what, like a thousand times. I'm not interested in going to a rave. I'd rather have a stick in my eye." She massaged her forehead with her free hand as she remembered how the whole mess started.

Two months ago, Jodi and Heather, along with six other honor students from the junior class of Fort Washington High School in Huntingdon Valley, Pennsylvania—Stan "da Man" Taylor, Kat Koffman, Bruce Arnold, Carlos Martinez, Vanessa Johnson, and Justin Moore—had shared an unforgettable spring break together on a houseboat as part of a social studies project.

Kat, who had the idea for this reunion of sorts, hoped everyone from the trip could make it. School was almost out and Jodi re-called how Kat couldn't imagine anything more exciting than to lose oneself in the laser lights and sound—away from parents, away from rules, away from the mundane drill of life.

In celebration of Memorial Day, according to the flier Kat picked up at Recycled Records, this event would be two raves in one. A Storm Rave would be on one side featuring a blend of German hard-core and jackhammering techno. Kat, as a seasoned raver, had explained to the group that the music at a Storm Rave pushed an insane 180 beats per minute. She admitted it was almost too fast to dance to for any length of time without, as Kat put it, "a little help." Jodi figured she was referring to speed.

But, Kat had been quick to point out that the other side would feature a Classic Rave with Happy House, in line with more of an electronic hip-hop, disco vibe. Something for everybody. The hottest DJs from New York, Detroit, and San Francisco were slated to spin the tunes for this twelve-hour continuous, dual dance party in an old, abandoned warehouse in downtown Philadelphia.

So far, Justin, Vanessa, and Jodi weren't going. Justin had a martial arts competition the next day and couldn't compete if he stayed up all night. Vanessa was helping her dad move to Pittsburgh and couldn't make it. But, according to Heather, Jodi didn't have a good excuse for staying home and, for the better part of an hour, she'd been lobbying Jodi to change her mind.

"Listen, Heather," Jodi said, "it's not like I'm judging you. But doesn't it bother you just a tiny bit what goes on at those parties?" She hopped off the padded barstool to rummage through the kitchen for a light snack.

"How would you know anything about raves if you've never been?" Heather asked.

Jodi opened the refrigerator door and glanced inside. "I read. I watch the news. I've heard stuff."

"Like what?"

Jodi spotted a slice of leftover cheesecake, but decided in favor of the bag of baby carrots in the crisper. She grabbed a handful and then returned to her seat. "You know, like the way some of the guys, well, they grope you while you're dancing and how drugs are everywhere . . ."

Heather cut in. "Doesn't mean you have to take 'em, too. Most people go to just dance and have a good time. Besides, Kat said the raves are all about that PLUR thing."

Jodi rolled her eyes. "Peace, Love, Unity, Respect—whatever." She started to eat a carrot.

"Something wrong with that?"

Jodi munched on her carrot for a moment. "On the surface, nothing, Heather."

"So what's eating you?"

Jodi took a deep breath, then said, "All I'm saying is that Kat was making real progress in her search for God, you know, coming to Young Life with us and stuff. I just think it would send the wrong signal to her about my Christian faith if I went, that's all." She heard Heather clear her throat on the other end. "I see. What you're really saying is that I'm being a bad example by going tonight."

Jodi cradled the phone between her left ear and shoulder. With both hands now free, she reached back to pull her blonde hair into a ponytail. "Not necessarily. That's between you and God. But if you go and something happens to Kat, I just think you and I will, like"—she paused—"I don't know, but it's bound to change things between us."

"So now I'm the bad guy?"

"I didn't say that, Heather. You're putting words in my mouth. I happen to care deeply about Kat's spiritual life. I'm sure you do, too. And I think she's super close to becoming a Christian. I'd be pretty bummed if we did something to confuse her when she's so ready."

"Well, nice speech. But like it or not, I still plan to go. In fact, Stan's coming by to give me a ride . . . we're only talking the hottest guy on campus. As if I'm gonna pass him up—*right*."

Jodi could hear the excitement crackling in Heather's voice, but she didn't say anything. How could she? What would she say? *I'm so glad you're starting to date a non-Christian football jock with a loose reputation. Hope you "make out" okay.* Besides, Jodi had already voiced her feelings about Heather dating Stan.

When Jodi didn't respond, Heather added, "Well, whatever you're thinking, maybe I'm not good enough to be your friend. Sorry to disappoint you. Good-bye."

A harsh *click* snapped in her ear. For a long minute Jodi stared at the phone.

✳ ✳ ✳

"Hey Mom, hey Dad." Jodi tapped lightly on their bedroom door, which was ajar. "Can I come in?" It was 9:55 P.M. and Jodi figured her folks were reading in bed. She leaned an ear toward the door.

"Sure thing, honey."

She pushed open the door and then walked over and sat on the edge of the bed.

"Oh, I've been meaning to remind you, Jodi," her dad said, sitting upright. His back leaned against the headboard and his green terry robe, open at the chest, revealed a white T-shirt. "Mom and I will be getting home late from Grandma's tomorrow. You're still welcome to join us."

Jodi shrugged off his offer.

"We might even spend Saturday night if she needs your dad to play handyman," her mother added. "We'll let you know."

"Sure thing. I'll try not to be too bored." Jodi smiled.

"So what's up?"

Unlike many of her friends at school, Jodi lived in a home where she and her parents maintained a pretty peaceful relationship. She enjoyed bouncing ideas off them, especially matters of faith. At one point in his life, Jack Adams had taken some seminary training. All Jodi knew was that her dad had a lot of wisdom, and that's what she needed right now.

"Something wrong?" Rebecca Adams asked, looking over the edge of her glasses.

"Well, yes and no. Remember how I told you that Kat and the others from the spring break trip were going to this all-night rave thing tonight?"

"Sure," her dad said, adjusting his pillows. "You said you didn't plan to go, which was a relief to us."

Her mom added, "We weren't big on the idea, either. I mean, don't those kids' parents care where they are at that hour?"

Jodi shrugged. "Actually, Mom, they probably figure it's an okay place for teens. The flier says it's an alcohol-free dance, and nobody over eighteen will be admitted. Sure beats a keg party."

Jodi's dad nodded. "Now, when we were in high school . . ."

"Oh, Jack. Let her talk," her mom said with a friendly elbow nudge. "So, what's on your mind?"

Jodi ran her fingers through her hair. "Well, tonight I started looking at that devotional book you gave me, Dad—"

"Refresh my memory. Which one?"

"By that C. H. guy . . ."

"Try C. H. Spurgeon. *Evening by Evening*," her dad added.

"Right. Anyway, when I finished, I felt, like . . . well, I felt this really strong burden to pray for Kat's safety." She started to lean on her left arm. "And, believe it or not, I think God wants me to go." She paused to gauge their reaction. Her mom spoke first.

"Isn't it almost ten already?"

"I'd just make an appearance, make sure Kat's all right, maybe take a group photo with my disposable camera. It still has a few pictures on it. Anyway, I'll be back by midnight. Can I?"

Her dad spoke next. "You really feel this is what God wants you to do?" When she nodded, he added, "Well, we trust your judgment, but I'd really feel much better if somebody could go with you. Want me to drive?"

Jodi gave him a pained look as if to say, Thanks but no thanks.

"I get the picture." Jack Adams crossed his arms.

"Come on, you know I love you, Dad." They traded smiles.

"Hey, I've got an idea," Jodi said. "Bruce is working late at the Pet Vet, you know, the one just around the corner. I think he's planning on going. Maybe I could catch a ride with him."

"I'm not so sure I like your being out that—," her dad started to say.

"Shh, I think it sounds like a fine plan," her mom said with a smile. "Just be careful, okay?"

"At least take your cell phone . . . ," her dad added.

"Call us if you need anything," Jodi's mom said. "We'll be praying for Kat, too."

Jodi hopped off the bed. "Thanks!"

"Well, dear, sounds like this'll give us the whole house in case we get a little frisky," her dad said with a wink toward his wife.

Jodi raised her eyebrows.

"Gro-o-oss . . . I think I'm leaving now."

Bruce carefully maneuvered his partially restored, 1969 Mach 1 classic Mustang through bumper-to-bumper traffic, although in his case both bumpers had been temporarily removed. Jodi wasn't into old cars, but listened politely as Bruce explained that the two-door coupe had been a gift from his dad when he turned seventeen back in April.

The radio didn't work, and the 8-track tape player hanging below the dash was useless. The seats needed to be recovered. And though reliable transportation, the body rust had been extensive. After hours of sanding the Bond-o and fiberglass strips, Bruce applied a patchwork of gray and red spot primer, depending on what the auto parts store had in stock. He'd have it painted once he saved enough cash.

"So where's the turn?" Bruce asked.

"Um . . . make a left on Christian Street, then a right on Christopher Columbus Boulevard—I think." Jodi was trying to make sense out of an old map. Her efforts were complicated by a malfunctioning dome light. She did her best to study the map with the available light from the street lamps that washed over the car as they drove. "Yeah, that's the way," Jodi said, pointing to his left.

Bruce turned onto Christian Street. "Gee, looks like half of Philadelphia is here," he said. "Talk about a party. I had no idea these raves were so popular."

"Me neither." Jodi glanced out her window at a steady stream of teens on foot. "Looks like we're gonna have to walk a few blocks. Let's grab the first spot you see."

"I'm all over that," Bruce said, followed by an easy tap on the horn for the benefit of a kid who started to cut in front of his car, evidently unaware of its presence. "Hey, check out what's in his mouth."

"I know. A baby pacifier. Weird," Jodi said, squinting. "And what's with the way these guys are dressed?" She nodded toward the sidewalk. "They're, like, oversize toddlers with Day-Glo face paint. I mean, half of them—correction, most of them—have pacifiers around their necks. That girl's sucking on hers, too."

Bruce drummed his fingers on the steering wheel as traffic slowed again. "And that's gotta be the fifth Sesame Street backpack I've seen in three minutes." He pointed to the right.

"I know." Jodi nodded in agreement. "Am I missing something here?"

He glanced over at Jodi for a second. "Beats me. I'm a newbie, too."

"A what?" She returned the glance.

"Newbie. That's what Kat calls a virgin raver. You know, a first-timer." He turned his focus back to the road.

"Isn't that special," Jodi said with about as much sincerity as the Church Lady on *Saturday Night Live*.

"They look like the kindergarten class on a field trip," Bruce said with a laugh.

"Yeah, or maybe they didn't get the memo," Jodi said.

"What memo?"

"That Halloween is over!" They shared another laugh.

Jodi folded the map and tucked it into the glove compartment. "Hey, it's nice of you to give me a lift," she said after a minute. "You sure it's okay that I've got to be home by midnight?"

"No prob, Cinderella. Wouldn't want you to turn into a pumpkin." He chuckled. "Just kidding. I mean, I can't stay long, either. Got to get to work in the morning. If I'm late, the dogs get restless and poop in their cages." He turned right on Columbus. "And I hate it when that happens."

"I can imagine."

Bruce shifted gears. The Mach 1's throaty muffler snorted as they picked up speed. "So why'd you decide to come after all? I mean, I thought you were kinda against the whole idea."

"Oh." Jodi hadn't anticipated that question. "Um, let's just say it's a God thing."

"I see, sort of like what happened on the houseboat." He was fishing for more, and Jodi knew it. She just didn't feel like going into details. She changed the subject.

"Yeah. Like that. So tell me about life as a big-time vet."

"Well," Bruce said, tilting his head to one side, "I'm not exactly in the big time yet. Just kinda learning the ropes. Mostly it pays well and I need the cash for this baby." He patted the dash. "But take my boss, Dr. Blackstone. Now there's a guy who's in the big time. Drives a brand-new, jet-black Porsche Boxster. You know what a little two-seater like that'll set you back?"

"No idea."

"We're talking $57,000 . . . that's decked out with the touring package, big wheels, the pimp stereo—you name it, he's got it."

"For real?" Jodi's eyes widened. "Kinda makes you wonder how a pet doctor can afford that kind of cash, doesn't it." Jodi looked over at Bruce, unsure if she had offended him. "I mean, don't get me wrong, but it's not like he's a dentist or a lawyer."

"We are, you know, a full-service upscale clinic," Bruce said, playfully sticking his nose up in the air. "Bring your pooch or kitty and we'll do their hair, nails, spaying . . . you name it. Why, Dr. Blackstone even does doggy braces for some clients."

"No way!"

"Yup. Imagine that." Bruce changed lanes. "Talk about being a real entrepreneur."

"Ooh. Big word alert!" Jodi said.

Traffic picked up again. Bruce glanced at Jodi for a second and said, "Yeah, anyway, I'll probably work for him this summer. How about you? You gonna get a job—or a tan this summer?"

"Do I look that pale?" Jodi looked down at her arms.

"I think a jar of mayo has more color—" Bruce paused. "Jodi, I'm joking."

"Um, right . . . but, yeah, I thought about doing an internship at the paper."

"Cool. We get the *Inquirer*."

"Actually, I'm talking about the *Montgomery Times*. They're just a weekly rag, but I like the local feel."

"Don't they specialize in like pet obituaries and church picnics?" He flashed a cheesy grin.

"Bruce, don't make me come over there and punch you one," she said playfully. "My dad says I've always had an eye for detail and, like, everybody's gotta start somewhere, right?" Jodi hooked her hair around her left ear. "I think it'll be fun. Oh, and I met the guy who'd be my boss yesterday. Seems real nice."

"Yeah, you'll do great. Speaking of bosses"—Bruce started to shake his head—"mine gets pretty ticked when things don't, like, go his way."

"Really?"

"Well, like, this week, we ran out of the usual generic syringes with the black plunger tips. Dr. Blackstone almost blew a gasket. Me? I can't see how that matters."

"Over there, on the right, three cars up. The guy's pulling out," Jodi said, pointing. "So, what were you saying?"

"Oh, it's nothing, really. Just that my boss can be a hard man to please." Bruce pulled his car into the now vacant spot and got out. "Make sure it's locked. You'll have to push the lock down and hold the button in while you close the door," Bruce said. "Pretty low-tech, but it works."

"Got it," Jodi said after the second try. They joined the flow of teens headed to the rave.

"Speaking of low-tech, what's that?" Bruce pointed to the disposable camera Jodi was carrying.

She laughed. "Yeah, I feel like such a tourist. I figured maybe we could take like a group shot, or something. Dumb idea, huh?"

"Why not?" Bruce smiled. "You just never know what might turn out."

Christopher Columbus Boulevard ran north and south, parallel to the Delaware River. The eastern edge of the street was to the left of Jodi and Bruce. It was marked by well-worn piers, an occasional building of some ancient vintage, and idle shipyards. Jodi could hear but not see the river water lapping against the docks.

They were heading south, which bothered her. The farther south, the farther away from the safety of Penn's Landing, one of the few recently remodeled piers that sported colorful shops, plenty of outdoor lighting, and a modern transit station where she could quickly take the EL 17 elevated train back to civilization. Instead, each step of their present course took them deeper into a landscape marked by decay.

Indeed, many sections of Philadelphia, the birthplace of the nation, had died the slow death of neglect, suburban migration, poor planning, and an upswing in the criminal element. This area was about as bad as any she'd ever seen—not that she could see much. Most of the streetlights were burned or busted out, leaving the buildings they passed shrouded in darkness.

In a few instances, thanks to the headlights of the traffic, she could tell someone had gone to the trouble of boarding up the windows and plastering the doorways with tired-looking NO TRESPASSING signs. And she noticed that the only fresh paint many of these buildings displayed came from graffiti artists marking their territory.

Even though other ravers shared the sidewalk, Jodi had the creeps and wondered if Bruce felt the same.

"Boy, this place is a dump," she said, breaking the silence. "My dad would flip if he knew I was in this part of town."

"Looks like a great place to hang out—if you're Freddy Krueger," Bruce said, then nudged her with his elbow.

"Cut it out, Bruce." She let out a nervous laugh.

"Come on, Jodi. It's really not *that* bad."

She shot him a doubtful look.

"Okay, so I wouldn't want to build a summer house here. You wanna head back?"

Jodi couldn't shake the feeling that they had to get to Kat. For what reason, she was unsure. It didn't really matter. Earlier she had prayed about it and felt God wanted her to go. She wasn't about to pull a Jonah and run from what she'd been led to do. "No," she said, "not as long as you promise to stay with me. Deal?"

"Hmm. Let me think about it . . . ." Bruce tilted his head to one side, pretending to be wrestling with his answer. "Okay, deal."

Still, the handful of strip joints, tattoo parlors, and men leaning against the hollow, vacant buildings intensified her anxiety. She quickened her steps.

"Hey, where's the fire?" Bruce reached forward and grabbed her arm to slow her down.

"Sorry. Guess I'm a little jumpy," Jodi said.

"What could go wrong . . . besides some psycho jumping us from one of those buildings?"

She punched him in the shoulder.

✳ ✳ ✳

It was 11:00 P.M. when the dark outline of the warehouse came into view. As they approached, they discovered that the enormous blood-red-brick building was situated on the river side of the street. Most of the windowpanes were shattered or missing. A rusted chain-link fence, topped with twisted strands of razor-tipped barbed wire, surrounded the warehouse.

They were within one block of the rave. From this position, the building took on an ominous air as laser lights from within reflected off the remaining shards of glass in the busted-out windows. Jodi thought it looked about as inviting as a medieval castle.

Hundreds of teens, she guessed, hovered outside. Some danced in place to the bass-heavy thumping of music, now more pronounced, which spilled into the street. Others, wearing surgical masks, hung on to each other as they staggered along like drunken sailors.

"Somebody's gonna have fun cleaning up this mess in the morning," Jodi said as they walked through discarded rave fliers and ditched cigarette butts littering the ground.

"Looks like a job for the Molly Maid Service," Bruce said, giving a kick to a beer can. "Hey, over there." He pointed to the left of the parking lot. "Looks like that's the way in."

"Through the fence?"

"You got a better idea?" Bruce said with a pull on her arm as he walked toward it. "See, everybody's going through there. It's already been sorta peeled back." He yanked her arm again.

"I'm coming already."

A moment later they stepped through the fence and, a short distance away, spotted four burly men at a makeshift wooden stand checking I.D.'s, collecting money, and hand-stamping those who paid as if they had just purchased a day pass to Disneyland. Beyond them, four more stood immediately in front of an oversize door with hand scanners, similar to the ones used at an airport security checkpoint, body-checking people before admitting them into the building.

Jodi and Bruce paid the ten bucks, got the security treatment, then walked through the door into a dark sea of pulsating, sweaty bodies. Overhead, laser lights spasmodically sliced the darkness, hammering the crowd with short, intense blasts of color. White gloves, worn by some of the ravers, reflected the laser pulses, while others waved Glo-Sticks in the air as they danced. Some had smeared neon paint on their faces and chests, like witch doctors, further amplifying the surreal scene.

They stood temporarily mesmerized, paralyzed by the barrage of audio and visual input. Bruce tapped on Jodi's shoulder. She leaned over to hear him above the near-deafening music.

"Dorothy, looks like we're not in Kansas anymore."

"You can say that again," Jodi shouted back. "What a zoo!"

They moved away from the entrance and walked along the back wall. As far as she could see, the room was about the size of a football field. Thick timber posts, each spaced about a car's length apart, ran the length of the building. She observed how each post supported rough-hewn beams on which the wood ceiling rested some fifteen feet overhead. Between the bursts of light she thought she saw portions of the ceiling sagging.

Bruce yelled in her ear. "Have you ever seen so many speakers?"

"What?" Jodi yelled back, now looking at him.

Bruce pointed at the sound system. The speakers were stacked almost to the ceiling on either side of the DJ, who, spinning vinyl records on matching turntables, was perched on scaffolding seven feet above the crowd. The DJ platform was bathed in flashing red, blue, and purple lights suspended from an overhead lighting rig.

"The speakers . . ."

She nodded. "It's crazy. I think I'm going totally deaf!" Jodi covered her ears to make the point. "How are we gonna find the others?"

"I know. Must be like a couple thousand people here," Bruce said. "Maybe I should jump onstage and make an announcement." He grinned.

"Sure thing, Tarzan," Jodi said. "Hey, wait a minute. Isn't that Carlos?" Carlos Martinez was one of the eight junior class students who had been on the houseboat with them over spring break.

"Where?" Bruce tried to follow Jodi's gaze.

"See that table . . . over there . . . the one with the balloons?" Jodi said. She pointed to their left about thirty feet farther along the back wall.

"Hard to say. I'm with you."

They worked their way through the crowd and approached the table. Jodi suddenly stopped. She shouted, "Rats. False alarm."

"That's not him?"

"Not unless he shrank six inches and got an earring since yesterday at school."

A girl wearing baggy jeans and a tie-dyed shirt waved to them from behind the table. Beside her stood several others who, like her, were selling balloons to other ravers. She held out a balloon and shouted, "Five bucks."

"For what?" Bruce shouted back.

"Whip-its."

"For a balloon?" Jodi asked.

"No, no. A Whip-it."

Bruce and Jodi just gave her blank a stare.

"See, you put it to your mouth and you inhale it. You go—" She gave a mock demonstration without inhaling. "You suck in the air as many times as possible."

"What for?" Jodi asked, puzzled. "To talk like Mickey Mouse?"

"For a thirty-second knockout. You know, like, the world stops spinning. It's really cool. Come on, come on. It's fun."

"I'll pass," Jodi said, waving her off.

She turned to leave when Bruce said, "So tell me how it works. What's in it?"

Jodi whipped her head around. "You can't be serious?"

"I'm just curious, that's all," he said, raising a hand, palm out as if to say, Trust me, I know what I'm doing.

She shook her head in disbelief.

Another worker behind the table leaned toward them. "Okay, let me tell 'em. It's just nitrous oxide—you know, it's like the laughing gas dentists use, only different. So when you inhale it, your lungs fill and it cuts off the oxygen to your head."

"That's supposed to feel good?" Bruce asked, his left eyebrow shooting up.

The girl with the tie-dyed shirt cut in. "Dude, then everything blacks out for like half a minute. It's totally out there. Try it. Come on, do it for me," she said with a mock pout. She held out a yellow-filled balloon for him to take.

Jodi tugged at Bruce's arm. "We're wasting time."

"Better not . . . Mama's calling," Bruce said with a laugh, then turned to leave with Jodi.

The girl called after him, "Are you sure? It's good stuff!"

Bruce pointed at Jodi then threw up his hands. "Sorry, gotta go."

Jodi was about to blast him for the Mama comment when a kid wearing a smiley-face T-shirt turned around, blocking their path. He took the pacifier out of his mouth and shouted, "You rolling?"

"Are we what?" Jodi asked.

"Rolling . . . are you, you know, trippin'?"

Jodi's face registered surprise.

"I'm on E right now, just took my second pill," he said, holding up two fingers, then added, "and I'm very, very happy." He took a step closer—a little too close for comfort. "That's my buddy," he said, pointing over his shoulder. "He's on four. Come on, let's party." He reached out to embrace Jodi's waist.

"Bruce!"

Bruce must have seen the panic written on her face. He pulled her to his side. "Hey, back off, pal," he said firmly.

The smiley-face kid staggered backward as if hit with a gust of wind. "Dude, what's with the negative energy . . . where's the love?" He waved them off in disgust, and then went to his friend for a pro-longed kiss.

Jodi winced. She turned away and faced Bruce. "Guess anything goes around here," she said, cupping her hand to his ear. "Thanks for stepping in."

"Sure thing. You know, I thought we could split up to look for the others, but after Mr. Liplock"—Bruce nodded in the direction of the boys behind her—"that's a lousy idea."

"I'm with you," Jodi said, relieved.

"I've got it," Bruce said. "Let's cut through the middle of the room to find the others. I'll look left; you look right. But let's stay together."

Jodi gave him a thumbs-up. Bruce turned and started to make his way through the mass of bobbing bodies. Jodi reached forward to rest her hand lightly on Bruce's back as he led the way.

They had gone twenty steps when a guy without a shirt, his bottom lip pierced with what appeared to be a fishhook, stopped Bruce and shouted something in his ear. Bruce shook his head no, then said something in return.

When the guy turned to another raver, Jodi tapped Bruce on the shoulder. "What'd he want?"

"He asked if I wanted some Special K. I told him we already had breakfast," Bruce said with a smile.

"What's Special K?"

"Beats me. Probably some kinda drug." He turned to go.

Jodi took several steps to follow when a pair of strong, slightly rough hands reached around her. One hand covered her eyes, the other wrapped around her waist. Together, the hands yanked her backward and didn't let go.

She couldn't see. Stunned, she tossed and squirmed, and bucked like a trapped animal. Even with her best effort, she found she couldn't break free. Who was this guy? What did he want with her? Was this some kind of joke? Her legs kicked as he dragged her away. She struggled to resist the arms that held her captive.

As she wrestled to get free, she had a flashback to the time she was ten, when her cousin Harry dunked her in the pool. His strong arms held her underwater until she thought her lungs would explode—just like now.

She gasped for air, and then shrieked—"*BRUCE!*"

Jodi hoped he heard her over the pandemonium in the room.

D r. Julius Blackstone stood perfectly still.

His steel-gray eyes peered into a specially designed, glass terrarium, home to his collection of prized tarantulas. He was completely focused on the drama unfolding before him. A dim, incandescent black lamp emitted just enough light for him to study their movements in the darkness.

When he drafted the plans for this terrarium, a unit measuring three feet wide, six feet long, and three feet tall, he envisioned a space to house three different varieties of tarantulas: his Usumbura Orange Baboon, an extremely aggressive, bright orange spider from eastern Africa that would strike if agitated in the slightest way; his King Baboon, an eight-inch African tarantula that, when peeved, reared up on its back legs to hiss; and, his personal favorite, the Goliath Bird Eater—the largest spider in the world with an eleven-inch leg span.

This somewhat hairy, orange king-size spider weighed, as he liked to tell children, "more than a McDonald's quarter pounder with cheese." Unlike the others in his collection, Goliath came from South America. When provoked, it would attack with its inch-long fangs.

He liked that.

He wondered how long Goliath would tolerate the little white mouse who scrounged around the feet of the spider, displaying no signs of fear. An instant later, Goliath was having supper.

Satisfied, he checked his watch. 11:15 P.M.

He closed and locked the door to his personal office, walked down a narrow hallway, and then followed the back staircase down to the basement. He punched in the alarm code for this restricted area, opened the door, and stepped into the lower-level operation suite. The only other access to this space came from an exterior door that, when opened, led to the back parking lot.

Dr. Blackstone graduated from Harvard with a master's degree in medicine. After Harvard, he pursued further education and training in the field of veterinary medicine. Now, fifteen years later, his Pet Vet Wellness Center, located in the heart of Huntingdon Valley, enjoyed a stellar reputation.

This two-story, state-of-the art facility sat on a gentle hillside surrounded by tall, mature pine trees. A level parking lot for clients, edged with colorful flower beds, was situated in front. To the right of the glass-and-stone structure, the driveway sloped downward as it wrapped around the building to provide employee parking and basement access.

Inside, five associates, three receptionists, and several interns processed the daily batch of pet owners who kept his waiting room constantly full.

None had any idea what took place after hours in the basement.

Dr. Blackstone stuffed the small, padded earpiece of his cell phone back into his left ear. The body of the phone was clipped to his belt. A three-inch microphone followed his jawbone, extending from the earpiece to his mouth. He spoke two words: Reverend Bud. The voice-activated cell phone dialed the number. It was answered on the second ring.

"You know who this is," Dr. Blackstone said. "No details. I'm on the cell. Answer me this. What can I expect tonight?"

Dr. Blackstone stroked his narrow black goatee as he listened. He rubbed his hands together back and forth as if anticipating a delicious meal.

"When can I expect your delivery?" he asked.

He had started to pace the white-tiled floor as he continued to listen when the sound of the exterior door opening behind him stole his attention. He'd been anticipating them. They knew the entrance code and were punctual.

"I've got company." He listened, then added, "Yes, our friends from abroad. Tonight, then. One hour." He abruptly terminated the call and turned to his visitors.

"Illya . . . Zhenya . . . Welcome."

Dr. Blackstone extended his hand to greet the Russians, first to Illya Kravchuk, the brains of the duo, then to Zhenya—whose last name was unknown to him—the brawn, although both men were pure steel. As he moved close to shake hands, his mind flashed back to a prior visit. He had taken them to Bally's gym for a workout and had never forgotten the experience; he witnessed their raw strength as they tossed the free weights around like two gladiators playing with plastic toys.

Neither man broke a sweat.

He recalled how afterward, in the locker room, Zhenya stood naked in front of the sink to shave his head. From the base of his neck down to his ankles, virtually every inch of Zhenya's muscular frame was wallpapered with tattoos: snakes, dragons, daggers, and females in various stages of undress.

When Illya stepped out of the shower, Dr. Blackstone noticed he, too, sported a similar collection of body art with two notable additions: the image of Saint Vladimir and a black widow spider.

But tonight, Dr. Blackstone observed, both men wore expensive black suits, charcoal gray shirts with gold cuff links, and shiny black shoes. Zhenya carried an unscuffed black leather case. No crosses. No body piercing. No facial hair. The only imperfection would be their broken English.

They shook hands, eye to eye.

Illya spoke. "Comrade Blackstone. How nice to see of you. You look well."

"As do you, Illya," Dr. Blackstone said politely, although he thought he detected a tension boiling beneath Illya's cold exterior. "Something to drink, gentlemen? A shot of vodka and a pickle? I have an unopened bottle of Stolichnaya . . ."

"Perhaps another time, Julius." Illya waved him off.

"Smoke?" Zhenya offered Dr. Blackstone one of his nonfiltered cigarettes.

"No thank you. But feel free," he said, knowing full well Zhenya would do whatever he pleased.

"Allow me to find point quickly," Illya said. "We are, how you say, without pleasure at situation."

Zhenya leaned toward his boss and said, *"Ti razacharoval menya."*

Illya nodded. He locked eyes with Dr. Blackstone, unflinching. "You disappoint us, Doctor."

Dr. Blackstone glanced from Illya to Zhenya, who at six-foot-one stood several inches taller, then back to Illya.

"What am I missing here? Everything is on schedule."

A long minute passed between them. Dr. Blackstone knew waiting was part of the game. In the stillness, he could hear the end of Zhenya's cigarette sizzle each time Zhenya took a deep, unhurried drag.

Illya broke the silence. "How important are your fingers to your work, Dr. Julius Blackstone?" Illya pulled a nutcracker from his right front pocket and cracked open a walnut. Pieces of the shell fell to the ground. He made no effort to pick them up.

"What are you saying?" Dr. Blackstone wiped the side of his chin with the back of his hand.

"What do you think?" Illya said, closing the nutcracker with a click.

Whatever Illya was driving at, Dr. Blackstone didn't have time to mince words. Preparations had to be made. Timing was everything and he had a tight schedule to keep. "You'll get your usual package— in the morning—as promised. Our agreement was cash money paid each time upon delivery. With all due respect, Mr. Kravchuk, I'm a busy man, not a bank. Do you have the money?"

A nod. "Zhenya, show good doctor bag of goodies."

Dr. Blackstone watched as Zhenya lifted the briefcase and held it in a horizontal position. Zhenya opened the lid. Inside he saw five rows of neatly stacked hundred-dollar bills. A wicked smile crossed his lips.

"Fifty-five thousand American dollars. If you like, count to be happy. There's much more where from that came, but alas, Dr. Blackstone, this is, um, the meat of the heart."

The heart of the matter—Dr. Blackstone was tempted to correct the metaphor, but caught himself.

Illya cracked open another walnut. The fallen pieces crunched beneath the heel of his shoe. "You said 'usual' package," Illya continued. "There is something about 'business as usual' that is, how you say, a snore? I much to prefer idea of business going up. *Mi poneali drook drooga?*"

It took a moment for Dr. Blackstone's limited Russian to make the translation: *Do we understand each other?* Sure, he understood, and said so. *"Poneal."*

No one spoke for a long minute. Zhenya took a final drag from his cigarette. He exhaled, blowing the fumes in the direction of Dr. Blackstone's face, and then dropped the butt to the floor.

Illya approached Dr. Blackstone and then reached around the base of Dr. Blackstone's neck with a powerful, viselike grip and squeezed. Illya lowered his voice a notch: "Do not disappoint no more."

They stared at each other—neither flinching.

"Nasha besyeda zakonchilsya." This conversation is over.

Illya turned and headed to the door. "Come, Zhenya."

Dr. Blackstone leered at the back of Illya's bald head.

Jodi swallowed hard. Her heart pounded against her chest with the force of a sledgehammer. Panicked, she had difficulty breathing. The more she struggled, the more the grip held fast, like superglue. Why couldn't she break free? What did this stranger want with her? Where was he taking her? Jodi felt his face nuzzle against her neck. She bristled.

"Don't fight it, babe." He spoke the words directly into her left ear, but the voice sounded muffled, even slurred.

Where is Bruce? she wondered. *Doesn't he hear me? What if he doesn't come in time?*

She screamed with everything she had.

"Brr-uuu-ce!"

Without warning, Jodi felt the arms around her go slack. She almost dropped to the floor. With some effort, she managed to stagger around and face her attacker. Her breath came in heaves. She wanted to run but felt compelled to see who the creep was.

As she stared, the darkness between them was intermittently pierced by blasts of laser light. A large, muscular guy wearing a Philadelphia Eagles jersey and blue jeans looked back at her. Something about him seemed vaguely familiar. But his face was covered by a blue surgical mask.

An instant later Bruce appeared by her side. "Jodi, you look like you've seen a ghost."

Jodi pointed at the guy with the jersey and shouted, "He attacked me—"

The boy hastily lowered his mask. "Hey, chill out. It's me—Stan Taylor."

Jodi's eyes widened in disbelief. "Well I . . ." She took a deep breath and crossed her arms. "That wasn't funny, Stan. How was I supposed to know it was you?" She glared at him. "I don't appreciate your—"

"You're way too uptight, kiddo," Stan said. "I'm just having a little fun here." Stan started to do a Snoopy dance in place. "Lighten up. You'll live longer."

Jodi's face felt flushed. She knew Stan "da Man" from school. Who didn't? As the star defensive lineman for the school's football team, which remained undefeated in the last season, Stan charmed his way into the hearts of students and teachers alike—especially the female students. Jodi had gotten to know him on the houseboat for the practical joker that he was.

She tried to say something witty, but she was too upset to think of a zinger. To her relief, Bruce changed the subject.

"Hey, what's with the mask?"

Jodi shouted, "He thinks he's Zorro."

"That's really funny, Jodi." Stan smirked.

"I'm serious; what's up with that?" Bruce reached out and touched the front of the mask that hung around his neck. "And what's that slimy stuff?" He leaned forward to take a whiff. "That's that VapoRub stuff. You sick?"

"Me, sick? No way. A little Vicks makes everything, you know, smooth," Stan said with a grin. "Like they say, Try it, you'll like it."

Jodi put one hand on her hip. "Tell me you're not rolling or whatever, Stan," she said.

"Hey, it's just one tab of E and a little Vicks. You know, sometimes you just gotta row with the flow."

Jodi wasn't sure if he was serious. "That's so not happening."

"Why are you jumping my case?" Stan said.

"I guess I didn't know you were a druggie." Jodi stared, both eyebrows raised.

Stan shrugged. "It's not like I do this all the time. Just sorta groovin' with the flow, Joe." He danced in place.

Bruce shouted, "You see any of the others?"

"Yeah. Heather's around here. Boy, can that girlie dance, know what I'm saying? Got that bootie shake happening big time." Stan elbowed Bruce with a wink. His eyes drifted over Jodi's shoulder. "Speak of the devil, she's over there." He pointed behind them, toward center stage, in the middle of the swarm of dancers.

Jodi turned around and was stunned to see Heather dancing hip to hip, then crotch to crotch with a bizarre-looking stranger. Heather wore a tight, white tube top and equally tight, hipster white jeans. Her clothes glowed with a purplish tint under the ultraviolet black light. Jodi's face flushed as Heather worked her body with an animalistic frenzy.

This was the same girlfriend who gave her heart to Christ at Windy Gap, a Young Life camp in Maryland, several years ago; the same friend who had just finished studying Romans 12 with Jodi last Sunday at church. *Whatever happened to "Do not conform any longer to the pattern of this world,"* Jodi wondered. She looked away sadly.

"She's got more moves than Britney Spears," Stan said to Bruce.

"Waa-ka Waa-ka," Bruce added, his head bobbing to the music.

"Are you guys done drooling?" Jodi asked. "I'd sure like to find Kat, you know?" She checked her watch: 11:37 P.M. They were running out of time before they would have to head home.

Stan put his mask on, inhaled, then asked, "You try upstairs?"

Jodi and Bruce exchanged glances.

Stan pointed to a doorway. He lowered his mask. "Take the steps up to the chill room. I thought I saw her there."

"The what?" Jodi shouted as the DJ ramped up the volume.

"Chill room . . . She's probably hangin' low, you know, just trippin' out—"

Alarmed at the thought that Kat might be doing drugs, Jodi grabbed Bruce by the arm. "Bruce, let's go—"

Stan blurted out, "Hey, what gives? You her baby-sitter now? Come on, I say let's *party* . . . she's a big girl."

Jodi threw Stan a disgusted look.

Stan said, "Why do you always have to rescue Kat, Jodi?"

"We'll talk about this later, okay?" Jodi's voice rose a notch. "Bruce, you coming?"

A fresh wave of urgency washed over her as she considered the situation. She hoped Kat wasn't so stupid as to take such a risk. Certainly not now—not after all they had gone through to save Kat's life just two months ago on the houseboat. The memories came flooding back as she and Bruce worked their way through the crowd to the stairway.

Kat had an accident, lost both kidneys, and would have died—except that Jodi, who had the same blood type, gave Kat one of her kidneys. That act saved Kat's life and left Jodi with one less vital organ. Donations like that weren't as casual as tossing coins in a Salvation Army bucket at Christmastime. This had been a major decision on Jodi's part—and a major sacrifice.

Jodi had been convinced that the temptation to party at the rave might be too great for Kat to pass up. As it was, Kat had to take special medication so that her body wouldn't reject the kidney. Jodi knew if Kat was so foolish as to take any substance—legal or otherwise, unless prescribed by the doctor—her body would probably go into a seizure. That's why Jodi had been so opposed to the whole rave idea from the beginning.

It was also why she was now running, pushing people who blocked her path out of the way. She had a sinking feeling that Kat was in serious trouble. *Maybe that's why I felt God wanted me to come tonight,* she thought.

A minute later they started to climb the well-worn wooden staircase. A kerosene lantern hung from a rusty nail. In its meager light, Jodi saw that the steps were covered with a layer of dried bird droppings. Pigeons, she guessed. Although tonight the music probably drove them away from their overhead perches, by the looks of it this place was home to a whole flock of the annoying little creatures.

She pressed on, hoping *not* to find Kat upstairs.

As she climbed the steep steps, Jodi thought she felt a spider web brushing against her face. The last thing she wanted to do was to accidentally step into their dusty mesh. She hated spiders—thanks to Mr. MacQueen, her tenth-grade biology teacher who made the class dissect an assortment of arachnids for two weeks straight. Her skin started to crawl.

Like a blind man with a cane, she swatted at the air in front of her, hoping to avoid contact with any cobwebs. Halfway up several teens were slouched against the side wall, sharing a smoke. A strong whiff of a distinctive odor—marijuana, of that she was sure—filled the air. She coughed as she stepped around them.

At the top of the stairs, Jodi entered the room. Bruce was several steps behind her. Her eyes had to adjust to the virtual darkness as only one temporarily rigged lantern cast a flickering yellowish glow against the bare red-brick walls.

Jodi squinted as she scanned the room for Kat. She guessed there were almost a hundred teens inside. Most sat on the floor. Some leaned against the wall. Some had Glo-Rings around their necks. Several passed around small, porcelain hashish pipes.

Jodi hugged herself. The chamber felt clammy; it smelled of must, urine, and burning plastic. She figured it was about ten times the size of the two-car garage at home.

"I've smelled better armpits," Bruce said, catching up to her. "At least it's not so loud up here."

He was right; the music wasn't as unbearable. Still, the floor vibrated as the bass-heavy thumping below hammered away at the floor joists with the intensity of a battering ram.

"Any ideas?" Jodi asked. "We really don't have much time."

"Who did Kat say she was going as?"

Jodi thought for a second. "Tinker Bell. Yeah, from that Disney movie—"

Bruce interrupted, "*Dumbo.*"

"Hey—I didn't deserve that." Jodi punched him in the shoulder.

"No, that's the name of the movie—*Dumbo*—isn't it?"

"Try *Peter Pan.* Anyway, she said she was gonna wear, like, pink pants and . . . oh yeah, she painted her white sneakers with glow-in-the-dark pink dots or something."

"Got it. So we look for a 120-pound fairy," Bruce said. "I say we head toward the far wall and work our way back."

"Go for it."

Jodi followed Bruce, stepping over several teens and around others, as they searched for Kat. They reached the outside wall where a little additional light from the street lamps below crept through the busted-out windowpanes. Jodi felt pieces of broken glass crunch under her shoes as they searched.

Still no sign of Kat.

Bruce turned to his right and snaked his way through the bodies. Jodi started to sweat; the room was as poorly ventilated as it was poorly lit. *This is insane,* she thought. The entire crazy setup: kids popping pills like candy while others dealt drugs in plain view. No adults anywhere. No police. No medical help. *What gives, not even a bathroom?*

For the first time Jodi was starting to seriously rethink her decision to come. Maybe God hadn't prompted her to go after all. Maybe she'd just imagined the whole thing. Maybe it was just her own curiosity. *A wild-goose chase,* she thought. *That's all this is.* She decided they should just call it quits.

Still ahead of her, Bruce turned to yell over his shoulder.

"Jodi—over here!"

Reverend Bud hadn't taken a shower in a week. Not that he was a once-a-day shower type, but under usual circumstances he'd manage a shower at least three times in seven days. But tonight, with its hot and unseasonably humid conditions, as he drove the sixteen-foot Ryder truck through Huntingdon Valley, his T-shirt clung to his thin rib cage, his shoulder-length hair remained clumped and knotted, and his scraggly beard itched.

It didn't help matters that the air conditioning was busted. But as long as he had his music he remained cool. Presently, Farley Funk's "Jack Your Body" filled the truck's cab. His homemade collection of house music from the mideighties was still his favorite tape. With his arm resting on the driver's door, the window down, he tapped the steering wheel in time to the irregular drum beat. He sang along with the track: "j-j-j jack your body."

He came to a stop at the traffic light on the corner of Philmont Avenue and Huntingdon Valley Pike. He took one last slow toke on the joint pinched between his thumb and forefinger, and then pitched the remaining stub out the window. He held his breath for a long moment, then exhaled.

He sat back, waiting for the light to change, but noticed the inside of the windshield had become lined with a greasy film from smoking. He wiped it with the side of his hand, which only served to smear the hazy substance in circles. The light still red, he tapped his horn once, and then rolled through the intersection.

A green duffel bag rested on the black vinyl seat next to him. He glanced over at it and sang, "j-j-j jack your body" again. He focused back on the road in time to see a police car approaching in the oncoming lane. After it had passed, he glanced in his side mirror and watched the cop disappear into the dark.

Up ahead his destination came into view. Without the use of his turn signal he veered left into the sweeping driveway and followed the parking lot around behind the building. With surprising care, he backed the truck into the loading dock. He shut off the engine, but left the tape playing as the gospel-sounding "Love Can't Turn Around," another classic tune, bounced out of the speakers.

Reverend Bud picked up his cell phone from the bench seat, pushed *01, and listened. It rang once. He said, "Dude, I'm here. Got the package just like you wanted, but I've been thinking—" He listened again, then said, "Cool, I'll sit tight." He pushed the END button, rested the phone on his left leg. He tugged at his matted beard as he waited.

A minute later, he heard the sharp cracking sound of the double doors opening behind him on the loading dock. He then felt the truck pitch back as an unseen worker stood on the back bumper to open the rear cargo door. He knew they'd take just a fistful of minutes to finish, and he'd be on his way.

He settled back against the headrest and closed his eyes. His body was relaxed, mellowed from the constant flow of stimulants he used during his daily routine. Yet the drugs did little to settle his spirit. He heard footsteps approaching his truck door.

"Please kill that music." Dr. Blackstone spoke the words evenly. "You know I can't stand it."

Reverend Bud didn't immediately open his eyes. He reached forward, eyes still closed, and lowered the volume.

"Dude, what, like no 'hello' . . . no 'How are you?'" Reverend Bud sat upright and looked out the window at Dr. Blackstone.

"How's the crowd?"

"Okay, you know something, Dr. B.? With you it's all business. I guess I forgot. The crowd? Yeah, we're styling. Biggest gig ever. Nice vibe. Lots of love. Lots of . . ."

"A number would be more to the point."

"Right. I'd say we're talking seven thousand smiley, happy people."

A devilish smile crossed Dr. Blackstone's face. "Let's have the cash. I've got work to do." He extended his right hand; his fingers beckoned Reverend Bud to hurry.

"Oh, yeah. The cash." Reverend Bud reached for the duffel bag. He handed it through the window. "Here's your bread, Dr. B."

Dr. Blackstone unzipped the bag and scrutinized the contents. He appeared to take a long whiff of the money, the aroma of which brought another smile.

Reverend Bud put his hand to his ear. "So like, I'm thinking there must be a 'thank you' somewhere in there?"

Dr. Blackstone zipped up the bag, ignoring the question. "When can I expect your main delivery tonight?"

Reverend Bud ran his fingers through his hair. "You're so welcome. Probably by three-ish." He leaned out the truck window. "But hey, I've been thinking, man. You know, I'm not real sure about all that anymore—"

"You better not say what I think you're going to say."

"Awe, come on, Dr. B. I'm just finding it a little over the top to . . . you know . . . I mean, we didn't start out this way. Dude, ever since those crazy Russians showed up—"

"Let me break it down for you." Dr. Blackstone waved him off. "I aspire to greatness. To success. To amassing wealth. In my view, you either drive the truck down the highway of life—or settle for becoming roadkill."

Reverend Bud bobbed his head as if he had heard the speech a thousand times before. "Yeah, but what I'm trying to say—"

"May I continue?"

Reverend Bud shrugged. "Please do, my man . . . whatever."

"When I found you, you were nothing more than a strung-out, small-time operator. A real punk. And your dad was a two-bit country preacher out in Clackertown—"

"Dude, it's *Quaker*town . . . and leave my old man out of it."

"—and he didn't have time for you, did he? Too busy saving souls, wasn't he? Had a hard time feeding your family, too, as I recall."

"Wow, what you're doing is so uncool, man." Reverend Bud looked straight ahead, shaking his head. "You've got some really bad karma happening."

"Look at me," Dr. Blackstone barked. "If you're so tight with your *old man*, why were you in such a hurry to run away? Listen. I'm the best thing you've got. I showed you the ropes, made you big money—lots of it. And there's more than you can imagine within your reach. If I were you, son, I'd lay off the ecstasy and find some 'smart pills' real fast."

Dr. Blackstone let the words hang in the air for a long moment. He added, "We've got a good thing going here. Plenty of other twenty-seven-year-olds would die to be in your shoes. So don't screw it up with your platitudes . . . or that tofu spinal cord." Dr. Blackstone sneered as he spit out the words.

Reverend Bud swallowed hard. "I hear you, I hear you loud and clear. But answer me this, man. When did you chuck your commitment to PLUR? Huh? Like, when did you sell out?"

Dr Blackstone shook his head. "Don't you get it? No, I don't suppose a seventies retread like you would understand. I don't care a rat's butt about PLUR. We've got to deliver, on time, as promised. Got it?"

Reverend Bud's eyes widened. "So it's the Russians, isn't it? I knew it, man. You haven't been the same since—"

"Don't *you* worry about the Russians. I'm perfectly capable of handling them," Dr. Blackstone said, his jaw tight. "You stick to your end of the arrangement . . . and nobody will get hurt. I'll expect your next delivery by 6:00 A.M."

Reverend Bud took a deep breath. He dropped his head back against the headrest.

Dr. Blackstone's jaw remained clenched. "Now get going—before I kick your hippie behind."

W hat is it, Bruce?" Jodi raced to his side and gripped his arm. He was standing six feet from a corner of the room where the outside and inside walls intersected. The lighting was especially sparse. His attention was fixed on several bodies slumped together on the ground.

"I think that's Kat," he said, pointing. "See her shoes? Her legs are kinda pinned under that guy there."

Jodi peered in the darkness. Her heart jumped. "Oh, dear Jesus— you're right! Look at her . . . she's a mess. What—what do we—" Before Jodi could finish her question, Bruce, who hoped to become a paramedic one day and used much of his free time reading up on emergency medical procedures, firmly nudged the boy whose body, lying facedown, was draped over Kat's legs.

"Excuse me . . . we need to get to my friend," Bruce said.

No response.

Bruce shook him again, this time more forcefully. "Hey . . . you mind moving over, pal? My friend needs help."

Nothing.

"He must be totally stoned," Jodi said. "Just roll him out of the way!"

"All right . . . you take his feet. I'll take his arms. Lift on three, okay?" Bruce counted to three; they lifted the boy off of Kat, turned him over, and laid him on the ground. He felt cold to the touch. Face up, Jodi noticed the boy was wearing a white T-shirt with a large, yellow Tweety Bird in the center. She also detected a used hypodermic needle on the floor where the boy had been lying.

"Bruce . . ."

"I see it." Bruce picked up the needle and studied it for a quick second. He placed it in one of the numerous external pockets of his green army fatigues.

"Why'd you take that?" Jodi asked as she rushed to kneel beside Kat.

"I'll have Dr. Blackstone take a look at it."

"Who?" The smell of vomit mixed with blood assaulted Jodi's nose. She had to fight the urge to gag.

"My boss. I don't know, maybe he can tell me what this kid was shooting."

Jodi placed her hand on Kat's sweaty forehead. It felt hot to the touch. Too hot, she thought. Not good. No way was this reaction from exhaustion. They needed to get her to a hospital, and fast. What she wouldn't give for a washcloth and some cool water to reduce Kat's temperature in the meantime.

She slipped her arm around Kat and propped her up against the wall. As she did, a syringe rolled into view. Jodi picked it up. Just what she was afraid of: Kat must have fooled around with drugs. Jodi closed her eyes briefly and shook her head. *How could you do something so incredibly stupid, Kat?* she thought.

Torn between compassion and the desire to wake up from the nightmare, Jodi shouted at Kat, "Look what you've done. Face it. You screwed up, big time. What are you on?" She held out the hypodermic needle as if it were the smoking gun of a crime, and then put it in her purse. She'd give it to the doctor at the hospital—if they made it in time.

Kat's lips started to move.

Jodi leaned forward, her ear close to Kat's mouth. She strained to understand Kat's slurred mumbling but nothing made sense. Jodi shook her head in disbelief.

So why am I wasting my time again? Jodi thought. *If Kat makes it through this, she'll probably just go out and get trashed all over again.* Jodi was mad enough to just walk away. Maybe Stan was right—she wasn't Kat's baby-sitter.

As Jodi wiped Kat's matted hair away from her face, a new thought surfaced. How many times had Jodi disappointed God? Did he ever give up on her? And what about the good Samaritan? Was she no better than the religious elite who avoided helping someone they felt didn't deserve to be helped? She bit the inside of her lip as she considered the implications.

"Bruce! Give me a hand with Kat. What do we do?" As she cradled Kat, she saw Bruce pull a penlight from his pocket and use it to study the boy, a kid of probably seventeen, she guessed. With his right hand, Bruce felt the side of his neck, then his wrist. He looked up at her.

"Use her A.A.O. to determine her L.O.C.," Bruce shouted back.

"English, Bruce. I'm no doctor."

"Right. Is she awake?"

Jodi searched Kat's face in the ill-lit room. "Kinda. Her eyes are open but sorta glazed over."

"Is she alert?"

Jodi waved her hand in front of Kat's eyes. "Not really."

"Okay, then she won't be oriented, either." Bruce lowered the boy to the floor, and then moved alongside Jodi. "Here, let me check her ABCs."

"Her what?"

"The basics: airway—breathing—circulation. First we've got to make sure her airway isn't blocked," he said, using his penlight to examine her throat and nose. "She's all clear. And she's breathing on her own. It isn't steady, but she's getting air. No external wounds or external bleeding."

"But she's so, like, hot when I touch her."

Bruce nodded. He felt Kat's forehead with the palm of his hand. "Not good. Her head's hot enough to fry an egg."

"Come on, Bruce, we've got to call 911. Here. Take my cell." Jodi fished it out of her pocket and held it out to him. "Take it. You'll know what to say . . ."

"Forget about it."

"Bruce, you crazy? Make the call."

"And give them what address? The fourth abandoned warehouse with all the busted windows on the left? In case you didn't notice, this place doesn't even have a name. And how would they find us in this crowd?"

"But we've got to at least try."

Bruce took the phone from Jodi's extended hand. Punching in the three digits, he cleared his throat and thought of how best to describe what was going on here. But there was nothing—no connection, no 911 operator asking what his emergency was.

Shaking his head, Bruce said, "I don't know why, but it's not going through."

Jodi's eyes widened. "What are we going to do?"

"We drive. We take my car. It's the fastest way. Here, let's lift her up. Put her left arm over your shoulder. I'll take the right."

"But what about him?" Jodi pointed to the guy in the Tweety Bird T-shirt.

"I couldn't find a pulse. I think he's . . . well, as far as I can tell, he's dead."

Jodi hooked her hair around her right ear. "Sounds like you said dead. Dead tired, right? He's just passed out?"

"I'm saying the guy has no vital signs. And he's pretty cold to the touch. Come on, give me a hand with Kat."

Jodi froze. This couldn't be happening. What kind of bizarre dream had she stepped into? Her pulse, already zooming, kicked into hyperdrive. Her mind raced. They needed to get the boy help, too. But how? Or, worse, was it too late for him? Could he, lying just three feet from her, really be dead? If so, they were in the middle of a crime scene.

So now what? She felt dizzy, disoriented. The music seemed to pound the floor beneath them with an angry intensity. The walls of the dimly lit room started to close in on her. She felt suddenly lost in a dark cave.

"What are you waiting for?" Bruce snapped.

"Hold on a second," Jodi said. "I've . . . I've got to do one thing."

On instinct, maybe from watching an occasional episode of *COPS*, she took her disposable camera, thankful it had a flash, and snapped several quick photos of the boy. His face. His torso. His full profile. Why? She wasn't sure.

It just seemed the right thing to do.

J odi sat on the ground outside the warehouse cradling Kat as if cuddling a wounded bird. Kat's body shook like a leaf in the wind. Jodi felt powerless to do more than pray and repeat, "Hang in there, Kat . . . you'll be fine . . . I promise you're gonna make it . . ."

She wasn't sure if Kat understood her. Ever since she and Bruce had dragged Kat out of the building, Kat had done little more than moan—a deep groan as if the pain flowed from the core of her being.

"I'm right here, Kat," she said, gently rocking her.

She wished Bruce would hurry. She checked her watch—again. She calculated that twelve minutes had passed since he ran to get the car. *What's taking him so long?* she wondered. *Maybe he forgot where he parked it. Maybe the car wouldn't start. What then?*

Inside, the music had stopped while a new DJ prepared to take over the turntables. Jodi, thankful for a break from the constant noise, heard him shout something into the microphone about being the "vinyl messiah" ready to lead the dancers into the promised land. The seemingly insatiable crowd squealed with delight at his self-proclaimed godlike status.

She looked up and scanned the parking lot for any sign of Bruce. Instead, she caught a glimpse of Carlos Martinez, at least she thought it was him. As he stepped into the light by the ticket booth, just twenty steps away, she studied his face. It was him.

Just then a boy holding a Kermit the Frog stuffed animal

approached Carlos. She watched as Carlos slipped him a small packet with white powder. The boy in turn handed Carlos some cash, which he promptly added to a large wad of money. Carlos tucked the money roll into a black leather fanny pack that hovered in front of his belt buckle. The boy, holding his frog and what she was convinced were drugs, went inside.

Jodi cupped her hands around her mouth and called his name.

Carlos turned, looked at her, and then walked in her direction. She could tell by his expression as he approached that he didn't recognize her. He stopped and stood three feet away. His head leaned slightly to one side. His thin, all-purpose smile revealed a gold tooth cap, which complemented his gold bracelet, two gold chains around his neck, and four gold nugget rings, two on each hand.

"It's me, Jodi Adams . . ."

"Oh yeah, sure. Hi. Pretty awesome party, huh?" Carlos said to Jodi. He glanced at Kat.

Jodi was in no mood for small talk. "You dealing these days?"

His right eyebrow shot up. "Whatcha need? E? Calvin Kleins? Supernovas? Special K? I gotcha covered. I just didn't take you to be, well, the type, you know?"

"I'm not . . . and that makes two of us, Carlos." Her tone took him by surprise. "Since when did you become a drug dealer?"

"Hold on a minute." He held up his hands palm out as if surrendering. "There's way too much baggage with that term. I'm a facilitator of good times," he said with a cheesy smile. "I much prefer the term 'vibesman.'"

"You're so clueless, Carlos." Jodi stared at him until he looked at his feet. Although she didn't know Carlos very well, she pegged him as being sensitive to other people's pain. Now she wasn't so sure. Didn't he see the condition Kat was in? Was he so full of himself that he didn't notice her suffering? Or worse, perhaps he didn't care. "H-el-l-o-o . . . ," she said. "Maybe you should take, like, a good look at Kat."

He stole a quick look. "Hey, don't blame me. I don't remember selling her anything. And, what if I did?" He swallowed hard. "I just give people what they want, you know—the good vibes and all that. Escape . . . happiness . . . whatever they want to feel . . . I make their desires come true. It's up to them to be responsible—"

Jodi wanted to sock him in the stomach. "So that's what you'd say to Kat and to the *dead* kid upstairs in that . . . that chill room or whatever."

"What are you talking about?"

"When Bruce and I found Kat, the boy next to her was dead."

He rolled his eyes.

"Don't believe me? Go see for yourself."

He shook his head slowly from side to side. "Come on, Jodi, maybe you're overreacting here."

"Give me a healthy break, Carlos. I'm telling you, he was dead. D-E-A-D."

"Well, I highly doubt that. Maybe he was just passed out, you know. Happens all the time. He probably just needed a nap."

Jodi waved him off. "Wrong-o. This guy needs a hearse. Bruce even felt for a pulse and couldn't find one."

Carlos shrugged. His eyes started to scan the line of partygoers entering the building.

Jodi reached up and grabbed his arm. "Like I said, who's in charge of this freak zone? Can't you see we've got to get Kat some help?"

Still distracted, Carlos said to Jodi, "Can't say exactly. All I know is I report to Reverend Bud . . ."

"A pastor? You're telling me—"

He looked back at Jodi. "No, he's not really a pastor. It's just a nickname someone gave him. He's like way into the whole PLUR message, always talks about it. He books the DJs and stuff. Come to think of it, he's sort of an evangelist of ecstasy, too. He's always passing out free samples of E. I started working for him a few months back. Nice guy, really."

The music inside started up again. Jodi yelled, "What's he look like? Where do we find him?"

"Ah, well, he's like pretty tall, kinda thin, he's got hair down to here . . ." Carlos pointed to his armpit.

"Color?" Jodi shouted.

"Um, brownish. And he's got a big smile most of the time. Oh, yeah, he likes to wear white T-shirts. I think tonight he was wearing his 'Got E?' shirt. At least that's what I see him in most of the time."

"So where is he?" Jodi pressed him again.

"Um, that's hard to say. He's here and there, depending."

"On what?" Jodi blew out a breath, ticked at Carlos's lack of directness. What was he hiding? Who or what was he afraid of? As she waited for a response, she checked the time. Bruce had left twenty minutes ago. *Where was he?*

"Carlos . . . depending on what?"

"Um, I have no idea. Like, he just rushed out of here about an hour ago. Said he'd be back sometime tonight. That's all I know." Carlos had a faraway look in his eyes as he spoke.

"Well . . . Gee . . . Let's see. Maybe you should tell him about the dead kid when he gets back," Jodi said.

He blinked and then locked eyes with Jodi. His tone turned suddenly serious. "Personally, I'd suggest you don't go around spreading rumors about dead kids and stuff. Let it go, you know?"

"Come on, Carlos. What's really going on?"

He jammed his hands into his front pants pockets, looked over his shoulder, and shuffled his feet.

"You know something that you're not telling me. Why not?" Jodi asked.

His face was tight as a drum. His eyes darted back and forth, like a squirrel scrambling to get out of the road. "Look, I . . . I've gotta go. People are waiting on me . . . and like I said, don't mess with it, okay?"

He didn't wait for her answer. He turned around and disappeared into the building.

Reverend Bud maneuvered the Ryder truck into the stream of traffic on Roosevelt Boulevard with the finesse of Godzilla. He didn't use his turn signal and he didn't wait for the flow of oncoming cars to clear before pulling into the right lane. Once in place he didn't accelerate, choosing instead to take his time. He was in no hurry to return to the warehouse, contrary to what Dr. Blackstone might have wanted.

Behind him an angry horn exploded with a rapid-fire series of blasts. In his rearview mirror he witnessed a man in a red pickup truck swerving to avoid a collision. Several seconds later the man pulled alongside the truck's door, shouting a stream of obscenities supplemented by a few choice hand gestures.

Without looking at him, Reverend Bud flashed a peace sign with his left hand. Instead, his focus alternated between the road ahead and the joint in his right hand. His cell phone chirped on the seat beside him, momentarily drawing his attention. He took another slow, unhurried drag from the joint and then rested it on the edge of the dashboard. He reached for the phone.

"Whassup?"

The noise on the other end of the phone made hearing difficult. He lowered his music. "Speak up, dude."

"Reverend Bud, it's Carlos."

"What's happening, my main man?"

"We may have a small problem—"

"Problem? With Jeee-sus, there are no problems. Only opportunities," said Reverend Bud with mock conviction.

As he spoke the words, his mind drifted backward in time. He pictured his dad preaching at the Quakertown Community Church. His father was, in his opinion, a dedicated man of faith, quite unlike the phony TV preachers he saw peddling prosperity and healing. He admired his dad's ability to touch people's lives, and he had been convinced at a young age that one day he, too, would become a preacher.

Ever since he was a child, Stephen Mason—his real name, a nice biblical name at that, although his dad called him "Buddy"—wanted to believe in a God of love. Yet he resented that this God required his dad to be away from home most nights. As far as he could recall, his dad was never able to take him fishing, to a ball game, or to the park.

By the time he was a teenager, he had emotionally withdrawn from his family. He lived inside his headphones. Music became his best friend. Two weeks after his seventeenth birthday, he ran away and ended up in a row house in Philadelphia with other dropouts. On several occasions he considered going back but wasn't sure how his dad would receive him. *Wow. That was ten years ago. What a trip,* he thought.

With time, Buddy discovered the rave scene and came to embrace the Peace, Love, Unity, Respect anthem as his personal creed. The drugs and mind expansion would come later. To spread the PLUR message, in an ironic twist, he adopted the role of "Reverend." Now, as the Reverend Bud, he preached PLUR. He lived PLUR. He introduced others to the PLUR message with an evangelistic fervor.

When he decided to promote his first rave, a modest success with local DJs, he found that he was a natural leader. Teens gravitated to his easygoing, welcoming nature. The crowds grew with time, although his events never attracted more than five or six hundred participants.

Until he met Dr. Blackstone and everything changed.

The larger crowds.

The DJs from the national circuit performing.

The underground drug market.

The Russians . . .

His thoughts were interrupted as Carlos squawked into the phone, "Hello? You still there?"

"Sorry, dude, must be a bad cell trip. Hit me again."

"Well, it's probably nothing but, like, this girl says her friend flipped on some bad drugs. Her buddy looked smashed. And she's all panicked. She insists there's a . . . um, a . . ."

Reverend Bud sensed the hesitation. "Yo, I get the picture. So who's this chick? She cool?" He took another hit from the joint.

"A friend from school, sort of. I mean I don't, like, really know her *that* well or anything. Seen her around. Anyway, she's pretty persistent . . . asking who's in charge and stuff."

"For real? She got a name?" He tugged at his beard as he listened.

"Yeah, it's Jodi Adams. She's not gonna hang around. Gotta get her friend to the hospital. But she may come back. Said something about going to the police, too. Just thought you should know."

"I dig." He switched the phone to his other ear. "That's one heavy trip. You know what to do, right?"

"About the—"

"Yeah . . ."

"Sure thing. Oh, and guess what else, Boss?"

"Wow, more good news?" Reverend Bud said with a laugh.

"You'll never believe who I saw a minute ago."

Reverend Bud exhaled a cloud of bluish smoke. "Let me guess. Old Saint Nicholas his baa-ad self . . . red jumpsuit, jingle freakin' bells, and happy glitter."

"No sir. Looked to me like your Russian buddies."

"Really?" He took a final drag, then flicked the butt out the window. "Major bummer. I'm tellin' ya, you don't want to share a lifeboat with those dudes."

"I hear ya."

"Okay, like, hang loose. Keep your nose clean and take care of things upstairs. I'll hit the scene in"—he tried to see his watch but couldn't focus on the dial—"soon. Asta pasta." With that Reverend Bud hung up. He set the phone on the seat and fidgeted some more with his beard. A minute passed.

He picked up the phone and dialed *01. It rang twice.

"Dr. B., so, like, why are Russians crashing my party, dude?"

Jodi was relieved to see Bruce zooming toward her. She had to raise her voice over the music, which, like a geyser, splashed outside the building. "What took you so long?" She started to stand, supporting Kat as she rose.

"I'll tell you on the way," said Bruce, gasping for air. "Left my car engine running. It's parked just around the corner. Let me give you a hand." Bruce helped her bring Kat to her feet. "How's she doing?"

"Awful. I'm really worried. She's messed up." That was an understatement. Several times Jodi thought Kat had stopped breathing, although she couldn't be sure. Jodi's palms were moist with sweat and her shirt damp with perspiration.

"Gosh, I see what you mean," Bruce said, feeling Kat's forehead. "We can make Abington Hospital in twenty minutes."

Jodi and Bruce walked as fast as the trio could go considering Kat, hanging like a dead weight between them, wasn't able to do her part. They stepped through the fence and then crossed the distance to the curb where Bruce had left his Mustang.

"Better climb in back. I'll put her in front," Bruce said, opening the passenger door. Jodi did as instructed. She squeezed into the pint-size rear seat. A quick minute later Bruce had Kat situated, her body on the floor with her head resting on the seat cushion. He hopped behind the wheel. As he peeled away from the sidewalk, Jodi was thankful to be leaving the warehouse in the dust. If she never came back that would be too soon.

"So, like, what's the deal? What took so long?" she said.

"Car wouldn't start. Had a dead battery. Must be a short some-where in the electrical system."

"Oh, that's great . . ."

"Hey—we're fine now, as long as I don't shut off the engine."

Jodi gripped the seat in front of her as Bruce took a turn a little too fast. "So how'd you get it started?"

"It's a stick shift so I popped the clutch."

"You lost me." She felt the power as the car lurched forward. The roadway was fairly clear and Bruce was taking advantage of the open road.

"My dad taught me an old trick. You depress the clutch while the car is in first gear. As it rolls downhill, you let up on the clutch while turning the ignition. The combination jump-starts the engine."

"But we didn't park on a hill."

"Exactly. That's what took so long. I had to ask some guys walk-ing by to give me a push while I worked the clutch. Took several tries, but we got it going."

While Jodi listened, she leaned forward to check on Kat. "Oh, I almost forgot to tell you. I saw Carlos. He's pathetic."

"Really? Like how do you mean?"

"You're not going to believe this—he was dealing drugs."

"Carlos?"

"Yeah. Must be making some serious cash, too. He had gold hang-ing off of him everywhere."

"That's nuts."

"Exactly what I said. Oh, and he was so, like, uncaring about Kat." The memory made her blood boil. "And get this"—Jodi sat forward in her seat—"I told him about that kid we found upstairs and he totally blew me off. Said I was imagining things. He didn't even offer to check it out."

She could still picture the teen lying on the floor, cold and unmoving in his Tweety Bird shirt. If only there were a police station, or even a passing police car, she'd at least be able to report him to the authorities.

"Speaking of drugs," Bruce said, pumping on his brakes to slow down for a stoplight, "I've been thinking about that syringe we found. The one by the stiff."

He looked up in the rearview mirror. Their eyes met.

"That's a crass way to refer to him, Bruce."

"That's what he was. Anyway, remember how I told you we got a zillion new syringes at the pet clinic without the standard black plungers?"

"Yeah . . ."

"You'll never guess what color they were." He paused. "They were red—just like the one the stiff, oops, um, just like the boy had used."

"I can't say that I see your point," said Jodi after a moment. "You think there's a connection?"

"That's what I can't figure out. See, like, right now, for example, we're spending a bunch of time making up batches of ketamine-filled syringes."

"Keta-what?"

"Ketamine. It's an animal tranquilizer. We use it all day long on cats and other, as Dr. Blackstone says, 'subhuman primates.' I'm told it's pretty lethal stuff if you're not careful. It even has a C-3 drug rating."

"Which means?"

"It's a class three, federally regulated drug," Bruce said. "Only a trained vet can use it as an anesthetic. Say you want to operate on an animal, you plunge the needle into a muscle." He demonstrated by jabbing his forefinger into his thigh. "Release the magic potion and, presto, the beast drifts into outer space."

Jodi watched as Bruce slumped forward, face against the steering wheel pretending to be knocked out—a stunt he could afford to do since traffic had come to a brief stop. He sat upright. "Seems we've carved out a neat little side business supplying other clinics with these syringes."

Jodi was genuinely interested, but was more concerned about Kat. "And the point is?"

He stepped on the gas again. "Well, you can't just walk into Wal-Mart and buy the stuff. So I'm wondering, like, what if someone broke into the clinic and stole some of our syringes?"

"Let me get this straight." Jodi ran her fingers through her hair. "You think that dead kid was shooting up with keta-whatever, which I don't understand since it's for animals, and you think he or someone, like, stole it from your clinic? All because the plunger was red, right?"

"I don't know. That's why I figure I'll ask Dr. Blackstone in the morning . . . just to be sure. You know, he could test the contents and—"

"You know what I think?" She didn't wait for an answer. "I think it's late and you've watched way too much TV."

He laughed. "You're probably right. Just the other day I saw this really cool special on—"

Jodi cut him off. "Bruce, pull over. Please? Over there by the police station." She pointed to a building two blocks ahead on the right of the car.

Ever since they had left the rave, Jodi was torn between her desire to help Kat and the belief that somebody ought to do at least something to identify the dead boy. If not her, who? She knew that after the rave was over and after everybody left, his parents would never know the truth about what happened to their son. The thought that his final resting place might be the second floor of an abandoned warehouse just didn't sit well with her. She had full confidence that Bruce would be able to get Kat the help she needed; he was, after all, a quasi-paramedic.

"You crazy? We gotta get Kat to the hospital."

"You can take her just fine. Me? I've just got to tell the police about that kid. And listen . . ."

"Yes—whatever you say, Nancy Drew," said Bruce as he pulled the car to a stop.

"Call me on my cell once she's there. I wanna know how she's doing, okay?"

J odi watched the red taillights of Bruce's car disappear in the night. For a fleeting second she had second thoughts. Although Bruce wasn't trying to be mean, his Nancy Drew jab had stung.

She was no detective, nor did she want to be.

Maybe she should just drop the whole thing. Of course, it was a little late for that option—now that it was after midnight and she had no car.

She turned and faced the two-story brick police station. She scanned the structure and decided the place must have been built by the Pilgrims. Thick ivy clung to the right side of the building, covering everything in its path from the ground to the bottom of the second-floor windows. Six well-worn steps led up to the towering, nine-foot oak door.

Jodi climbed the steps. She gave the door a shove with her shoulder; the hinges creaked a tired melody as it swung open. Inside, the place smelled of wet newspaper and dust. She took several steps into the room where a policeman sat behind a massive wood desk reading a paperback. His desk sported a phone, a pad of paper, and a pen.

He didn't look up or acknowledge her presence.

"Excuse me, sir."

While she waited for a response, she noticed the walls were painted a pale blue; peeling in some places, flaking off in others. Several feet to the left of his desk, a second officer in a folding chair leaned back on its two rear legs against the wall. His eyes were closed, his hands folded across his sizable stomach. Both men wore standard police-issue blue shirts and black ties, although this one's was loosened around the neck.

Jodi turned back to the officer before her and then strained to read his nametag. It read: Sergeant Schmidt.

"Um, sir. I hate to disturb your reading," said Jodi, annoyed by his lack of basic courtesy. "But I need some help here."

He turned a page and read some more before casting a look at her over the top of his thick, brown-framed glasses.

"Whatcha got that can't wait until the end of my break, sweetie?" He stuck a stubby finger between the pages to reserve his place.

Sweetie? Jodi folded her arms at the insult. "Well, with all due respect, by the looks of this place"—she uncrossed her arms and then placed her hands on her hips—"I guess I'm not surprised that a few thousand kids are stoned out of their minds at that rave around the corner." She pointed with her right thumb over her shoulder. She almost added, *while you're reading your book*, but didn't want to be disrespectful.

Sergeant Schmidt turned his head to the left and grunted, "Dexter, you still have your cape?"

"Cape?" Officer Dexter rubbed his face.

"Yeah, the one they gave you when you graduated from Superman Training Academy." Sergeant Schmidt burst into a blast of laughter so hard, he started to cough—a raspy, smoker's cough. He cleared his throat. "Listen, missy . . ."

"Jodi, Jodi Adams."

"Right." His jaw tightened, his face appearing pained at the interruption. Another grunt. "Ms. Adams, if what you allege is true—"

"It is."

"I'm sure *you* believe that is the case."

She shook her head. "I *saw* kids dealing drugs right in front of me. I was asked if I wanted ecstasy, like, probably four or five times. I know what I saw." Her hands were outstretched, palms up as she spoke.

He removed his glasses and massaged his temples. "Dexter . . ."

"Sir?"

"We got how many men on duty tonight in this precinct?"

"Let's see. There's me . . . and there's you. Yeah, two as far as I can tell."

Jodi was about to scream. "I don't believe this," she said under her breath. Sergeant Schmidt's hearing was evidently better than his vision.

"What's not to believe, missy? Facts are stubborn things and our hands are tied. We simply do not have the manpower to mobilize for a drug bust of that magnitude." He put his glasses back on. "And you can thank the mayor for that bit of reality. Now, if you don't mind . . ." He started to read his book.

Jodi took a deep breath. Her priority, after all, was the dead boy, not the flagrant sale of drugs.

"Actually, I'm here to report—or whatever—a dead boy."

This time the sergeant looked directly at her through his glasses. His eyes, like those of a walleyed bass fish, filled the lenses, thick as Coke bottle bottoms. She heard the echo of Officer Dexter's folding chair landing on all four feet across the room.

"That's a rather serious statement to make, Ms. Adams."

Jodi licked her lips. "Well, my friend Bruce and I both saw him—the victim, or whatever you guys call him. I'd guess he was maybe seventeen years old."

"When and where?"

"Tonight, at that rave I told you about. I don't know, maybe, like, thirty minutes ago."

"At the rave. Hmm." Sergeant Schmidt leaned back in his swivel chair, hands folded behind his head. "As a police agency we do not have the luxury of speculation. We deal in facts, as I'm confident you can appreciate."

She nodded in earnest.

He cleared his throat. "As such, I cannot have one of my officers climbing through abandoned warehouses sifting through garbage on a wild-goose chase. What makes you think the victim is dead?"

"We checked for a pulse and didn't find one. Plus, he was, like, cold when I touched him." Jodi rolled her head around her shoulders trying to release the throbbing at the base of her neck.

"Any sign of a struggle?"

"No."

"Any blood?"

"No."

"Any wounds?"

"No." She bit her bottom lip, sensing where he was going with this line of questioning.

"I see." Sergeant Schmidt made a fist with his right hand and used it to cover his mouth as he coughed. "Did you consider the distinct possibility that he was just sleeping?"

"With no pulse?"

"It's entirely possible you missed it. Frankly, people don't just die from dancing too hard." He had no smile. "Just making an observation."

Jodi started to respond, to tell him about the syringe they found, but he waved her off. "Listen, I can appreciate your sincerity. You're to be commended for doing your civic duty. We'll make a note of your report for the file."

File? What file would that be? He didn't ask for the location of the building, or the location of the boy in the building, or what he was wearing—or for that matter, even a basic description of the boy. *Jesus, what now?* she wondered.

"Excuse me, Sergeant Schmidt."

He grunted.

"I was just wondering if you, like, had one of those ride-along programs in this department."

His eyes narrowed as he rubbed the stubble on his chin.

Jodi continued. "I mean, the warehouse is just a few blocks away.

It's just on Christopher Columbus. Maybe Officer Dexter and I could ride over there, you know. I could take him right to the spot."

He scratched the side of his head. "This isn't the only case we're dealing with—"

"It wouldn't take but a few minutes," Jodi pleaded.

"Hang on . . . hang on." He turned to his left. "Dexter, feel like getting some fresh air? Maybe take her for a ride to humor her?"

"Sure, whatever."

Sergeant Schmidt rolled his chair back several inches, opened his middle desk drawer, and withdrew a single sheet of off-white paper. He held it up as if presenting a piece of fine art.

"This here is what we call our Waiver Form. Fill out the top part. Sign and date it on the bottom line." He slid it across the desk and tossed her his pen. "I'll need to see a picture I.D. . . . driver's license . . . learner's permit. Something along those lines."

Jodi snatched her I.D. from her purse, held it out for him to examine, and then tucked it back in place. She knelt on one knee and started to fill in the requested information on the edge of his desk.

"Keep in mind, by signing this paper you release us from all liability in the event of an accident, shooting, or other altercation that may jeopardize your safety. In other words"—he paused to cough—"we are not responsible for what may happen to you. Is that understood, Ms. Adams?"

With the help of two other workers, Carlos Martinez took less than fifteen minutes to completely clear the chill room. The ravers who had been partying, resting, or, in some instances, engaging in sex, were moved to a room in another section of the enormous warehouse.

Gone were the lanterns that had previously lit the second-floor area. Gone were any traces of recent activity.

Gone, too, was the body of the boy with the Tweety Bird shirt.

His task complete, Carlos began to provide stimulants to the crowd. He had sold product at several other raves for Reverend Bud, but tonight was by far the biggest score he had ever made.

Thanks to Reverend Bud working out the deal like a well-oiled machine, sales had been extraordinarily good. He provided the drugs and fixed the prices. Carlos and the others who, as Reverend Bud put it, "spread the love around" were permitted to keep 20 percent of everything collected. Sure beat flipping hamburgers for minimum wage.

Carlos, unlike the other dealers, never used the drugs himself. He preferred instead a clear head to work a little scam of his own. He found it easy to con or, in many cases rob, the stoned partygoers of their drugs. It was a simple task in the dark environment. He in turn resold the stolen narcotics and kept 100 percent of the profits.

And why not? Who would a raver complain to in the middle of the night? The police—who were never around? Even if the cops showed up, what could they say? "I bought some illegal dope and got ripped off"? Hardly. Carlos knew he was taking a risk, but the payoff was too good to pass up.

But tonight the encounter with Jodi had rattled him.

He had first met Jodi two months before. During their near-deadly voyage on the Chesapeake Bay he had watched Jodi put her convictions into practice, even at great personal cost. She wasn't afraid of self-sacrifice. And he came to see her motivation as being "into Jesus."

That made him even more uncomfortable, especially since his guiding principle was the motto "Every man for himself." You only go around once, right? Grab for all the gusto, even if that means taking from some loser who doesn't know any better.

Eat—or be eaten. Sure, it was shallow compared to Jodi's way, but it was his truth.

If he had any doubts about her sincerity, if he had wondered whether the whole houseboat experience was done for show, tonight erased all of that for him. The care for Kat's well-being that Jodi demonstrated was more than he could process.

Maybe there was something to Jodi's Jesus. Maybe.

He found it easier to shove the thoughts from his mind. Instead, he scoped the incoming crowd for his next transaction. Perfect. Two kids—definite newbies—had just entered. He wanted to get to them before the other dealers landed the score. As he approached them, Carlos passed two figures standing against the wall in the shadows.

Five minutes later, a hundred extra dollars were added to his private stash. He decided to step outside to see if Reverend Bud had arrived. He knew if his boss was around he would be hovering by the makeshift ticket stand.

Once outside Carlos felt a heavy hand on his shoulder. He turned around, half expecting to see Reverend Bud, but was surprised to be staring at a very large, bald man. Beside him was another unfamiliar face.

"Carlos, yes?"

The accent sounded foreign. Carlos squinted. "Do I know you?"

"My name is Illya. This is Zhenya. Please to walk with us." Illya's rock-solid hand wrapped around the base of Carlos's neck. He had no real choice in the matter.

"Actually, I'm . . . I'm about to meet with—"

"Carlos, first we talk, yes?"

"Um, sure thing. Um, like, so where are we going? I've really got to see Reverend—"

"No more words now."

Carlos felt himself carried along, very much against his will, across the parking lot in the direction of a train track. The track, which, in years past, had serviced the warehouse, ran parallel to the street about one block from the building. A row of now abandoned railroad cars remained parked in place. Zhenya reached up and opened a rusty sliding door to the middle car. They pushed Carlos inside before stepping in themselves.

Carlos, his heart about to burst, struggled to stand. He'd seen the Russians from time to time with Reverend Bud in the past. He didn't know the nature of their business and didn't care to ask. Now he wished he knew. Especially since they didn't appear to be the kind of guys who had a sense of humor: tight, all-business faces. Cold, narrow eyes. Moved with directness and purpose. He knew this was no social visit.

"Listen, um, guys. There must be some mistake here. I work for Reverend Bud . . . you can ask him, for real." Carlos felt beads of sweat roll down his forehead. The stale smell of urine, deposited by homeless drifters who used the railroad car as shelter, greeted his nose.

"Zhenya, door, please." Illya removed his nutcracker and cracked open a Brazil nut while Zhenya closed the door. They stood in the darkness as Illya cracked another shell open. The sound bounced off the hard, metal interior. A moment later, Zhenya flicked on a powerful flashlight.

"Carlos, in Mother Russia we say, *'Bez izvenenii.'* I believe American say, 'There's no excuse.'"

"Uh . . . the thing is, like, I really don't have a clue—"

"Shhh. I say you what I think," Illya said. "I watch you. Your fingers become sticky for money. *Our* money. Understood me?"

Carlos swallowed hard. They must know about his skimming from the drug money. But how long had they been tracking him? Just tonight? Or for the past several months? For the first time in his life, Carlos tasted a fear so thick he almost choked. Like a slow Internet connection, he began to piece together a picture of his situation. He realized he was in way over his head.

He couldn't run.

He couldn't fight.

He had no defense.

For a second, he wanted to concoct a story, something about a destitute mother, a brother who needed an operation—that's why he skimmed; anything to deflect the reality that he was in deeper than the ocean. And by the looks on their faces, that's exactly where he feared he'd end up.

"You think you clever man," Illya said. His right hand rapidly opened and closed the nutcracker as he spoke. The sharp *clack, clack, clack* sound of metal against metal made Carlos's heart race faster. Illya added, "Zhenya . . ."

The two men traded what was in their hands: Illya now held the flashlight, Zhenya the nutcracker. Zhenya grabbed Carlos by the forearm. His fingers dangled helplessly in midair. With a twist, Zhenya yanked the two gold nugget rings off Carlos's fingers and placed them in his suit pocket.

Zhenya then turned his attention to the two golden necklaces around Carlos's neck. Still gripping his outstretched hand, Zhenya stripped the fine jewelry from Carlos with a harsh, downward pull. He placed it, too, in his pocket.

Carlos thought the worst was over. They had what they wanted, right? They had the gold and they'd succeeded in humiliating him. He'd do anything they ask. So what more could they want?

Illya, still pointing the flashlight at Carlos, nodded to Zhenya and then sneered, "I say, Carlos not so clever no more."

Zhenya jammed the pinkie finger from Carlos's right hand between the jaws of the nutcracker but didn't clamp down immediately. His eyes remained riveted on Carlos.

Carlos, now aware of what was about to happen, fought in vain to pull away. He shouted, *"NO-O!!"* But he knew that the music from the party, which filled the air around this makeshift torture chamber, would prevent others from hearing his cry.

A nasty smile crossed Zhenya's lips. He snapped the nutcracker shut around the fragile finger. It cracked like a brittle twig.

Carlos roared in pain, his scream amplified by the harsh interior of the railroad car. The instant Zhenya released him, Carlos slumped to the wooden floor.

A minute later Illya spoke. "Nine left . . . not so bad . . . I make deal. You bring stolen money—all of it, Zhenya breaks no more. Seven thousand dollars. By noon, Saturday. But . . ."

Carlos whimpered, curled in the fetal position.

". . . if you no do, Zhenya will fix all nine. *Mi poneali drook drooga?*" Before offering the translation, Illya kicked Carlos in the stomach with the point of his highly polished boot. He struck with enough force to send Carlos's body briefly airborne into the side wall of the car.

"Do we understand each other?"

D r. Julius Blackstone finished his work in the basement of the Pet Vet Wellness Center—at least for the time being. With a click, he switched off the overhead light above the table. He pulled off his rubber gloves with a snap and tossed them in a chrome hopper. He removed his gown, face mask, and safety goggles.

He turned and studied his two assistants, who were likewise engaged in their postop cleanup. They had been handpicked by him, and he had full confidence in their skills. Naturally, he had personally trained them to be proficient in several key areas of expertise.

But were they trustworthy?

As far as he could tell, yes. Who wouldn't be for how he compensated them? That was the beauty of money. People would do just about anything—for the right price. They were no different from other greedy humans. And he always paid them under the table, in cash.

But still—were they trustworthy? The thought nagged at the back of his mind. How could he know for certain?

"Listen, I want plenty of ice . . . Ice is our friend," Dr. Blackstone quipped. "Frozen water is still cheap." He hung his gown and accessories on a metal hook mounted on the wall. "Kindly make sure everything is packed tight. I don't want anything leaking in transit."

"Yes, sir," said the older of the two assistants.

"As you can imagine, that would be a disaster on several levels," Dr. Blackstone said, stretching his arms. "Come to think of it, toss out the old shipping cartons. Use the new ones tonight. They're in the storage room. Make sure everything is red labeled."

"Got it. What time is the pickup?" the second assistant asked, scrutinizing his watch.

"About an hour, so time is of the essence," said Dr. Blackstone.

"We'll be ready, sir."

His eyes moved between the two helpers. "You'd better be." His tone reflected an edge produced by both his mood and his own exhausted state. Dr. Blackstone turned to leave but paused by the outside door. His voice softened slightly. "Get some rest. Tomorrow is a big day."

✳ ✳ ✳

Jodi collapsed in the backseat of the late-model, blue-and-white squad car. Her head rested against the window. She was thankful for its cool surface. She closed her eyes and wished her mind would stop replaying the last thirty minutes. *Talk about a real disaster zone,* she thought. She had never felt so embarrassed and stupid.

Officer Dexter drove the squad car back to the station without saying a word. Jodi's mind, try as she did to stop it, filled the silence with another painful instant replay. Upon their arrival at the warehouse, everything had appeared pretty much as when she'd left it: the bizarre-looking outfits, the sweaty bodies swaying in the laser lights, the ear-splitting music. If anything, the crowd was larger, and perhaps a bit rowdier, Jodi thought.

She and Officer Dexter had stood just inside the entrance, allowing their eyes to adjust to the darkness within. After several moments, Jodi pointed to a doorway across the room and to the left. Officer Dexter had grunted as he hiked up his belt around his waist and took the lead through the crowded dance floor. She had no choice but to fall in line, feeling as conspicuous as a baby duck following the lead of its parental unit.

The moment they began to climb the stairs she knew something was amiss. The lanterns in the stairway were gone, requiring Officer Dexter to use his flashlight. At the top of the stairs, she scanned the room in complete disbelief. She was dumbfounded to find it empty—with a capital *E*. She kept throwing her hands up in the air as if somehow the crowded room would reappear before them.

"You sure this is the right spot?" Officer Dexter had asked, huffing after the workout of climbing the steps.

"Well, I . . . yes, I'm positive. See that broken glass by the window?"

He trained the beam of light in that direction.

"That's where we found him."

"Who? The victim?"

"Yes. And . . . and over there were kids leaning against that wall smoking, like, dope or something plastic-smelling." She took several steps in the direction of where the kids had been sitting. She turned and faced him. "I mean, there were kids everywhere up here. You've just got to believe me—"

He scrunched his nose. "Then how do you explain—"

She shook her head from side to side. "I can't."

They stood motionless for a long minute. The music below pounded the floor with a *thump, thump, thump.*

"Miss Adams"—he cleared his throat—"you've had your fun; now we had better be going."

"Fun?"

"Well, the way I figure it, you dreamed up this whole dead boy story so as to get us down here." Officer Dexter had redirected the light into her eyes, now that she was the focus of his interrogation.

She squinted. "Um, and why would I do that?"

"Well, as I recall, you burst into the station all worked up over the drug situation and—don't get me wrong—I'm against drugs, too, you know. I appreciate your concern. However, like the chief already explained, our hands are tied—"

"May I ask what that has to do with—"

"See, his answer wasn't good enough for you, so as a ploy to drag us into this situation, you made up that story about the victim. At least that's the way it strikes me."

Jodi looked down, defeated. "So you don't believe me?"

He lowered the flashlight. His tone was all business. "Miss Adams, I have an obligation as an officer to maintain the integrity of any investigation. If that investigation starts with a fraudulent assertion of fact, well, let's just say we've got to drop it. In this case, the facts don't support your claim."

Jodi sighed now. The memory turned her stomach. She looked out the window of the police cruiser. To make matters worse, she recalled how she had met Reverend Bud as they left the warehouse. After accusing him of just about everything in the book, all he said was, "Hey, it took guts to bring the fuzz here."

"The fuzz?"

"Yeah, you know, the cops," Reverend Bud had said, nodding in the direction of Officer Dexter. "He must feel as out-of-place as a pig at a barbecue, you know what I'm saying?" He had laughed.

To his credit, Officer Dexter had ignored the friendly jab.

Then, of all the strange things, Reverend Bud had handed her a business card inscribed with his name, address, phone number, and the words "Peace, Love, Unity, Respect." Along the bottom edge of the card he had imprinted: *This Entitles the Bearer to a Free Tab of Ecstasy.*

What would she ever need that for? She almost tossed it on the floor. She stuffed it in her purse instead. She'd junk it later.

Right now, aside from the intense desire to crawl into bed and disappear under the covers, Jodi wished she could ask Phil Meyer what to do. Phil, the ex–Navy Seal husband of her social studies teacher, Rosie Meyer, had piloted the houseboat over spring break. He always knew how to handle any situation—at least that was her observation of the man. Talk about a rough character.

Jodi figured Phil could probably bust the rave single-handedly. She was tempted to call, but it was the middle of the night and she was in no mood to risk further embarrassment by waking him.

Besides, something else gnawed at her.

Why hadn't Bruce called yet? Surely he would have arrived at the hospital by now. Did he have some kind of car trouble? What if he'd stalled out again in that old car? She desperately wanted to know what was up with Kat. Were the doctors able to stabilize her? Was she conscious? More important, would she make it?

Jodi reached for her purse and took out the phone to examine it. "I'm such a dorkus," she said to herself.

It had been off the whole time.

* * *

Officer Dexter pulled the car to a stop in front of the police station. "Would you like me to call a cab for you?"

"Um, sure thing. Great. Thanks." Jodi opened her door and stepped onto the sidewalk. She thought about mentioning to Officer Dexter that Kat was in the hospital because of the monkey business upstairs. Surely Kat would be able to back up her story about the victim. Somehow the whole idea seemed like a waste of time now that her credibility was shot—at least in the officer's eyes.

Officer Dexter waddled around the car.

Jodi said, "Listen, about this whole situation—"

"Aw, don't worry about it. I was just busy taking a nap. These overnight shifts are murder, you know what I'm saying?" He smiled, and then added, "While you wait, we've got the world's best stale coffee inside if you'd like a cup."

"No thanks." His offer sounded about as appetizing as week-old cold pizza. "I'll be fine, really." She forced a thin smile.

"I'll call that cab. Good night, Miss Adams." He turned and left.

Jodi powered up her cell phone. It indicated she had two messages. She punched the icon for messages and listened. The first was from Bruce:

"Hey, Jodi. We're at the Abington Hospital in the . . . Excuse me, what building is this?"

She heard Bruce calling to someone in the background. His hand partially covered the mouthpiece.

"Sorry about that. We're in the Toll Pavilion. Gee, this sure looks like the same place Kat came to after her accident on the boat. Anyway, she's in room 210. They got her all hooked up to a zillion tubes and stuff. The doctor said she was seriously—"

The message stopped cold. *What's with that?* Jodi wondered. She waited for the second message to play.

"Jodi, it's me again. Must have hung up accidentally. Anyway, she's dehydrated and, um, in critical condition. She looks pretty bad if you ask me. They're running a bunch of tests, but it's too early to tell, like, what's going on. She's alive and that's a plus, right? Well, I'm going home now—hate to leave her, but visiting hours are over. Besides, I really need to grab some sleep. Like I said, gotta work in the morning."

Jodi heard Bruce fumbling with the phone as if he were about to hang up but then heard him add, "Oh, you know what's really weird? I heard Kat mumbling something in the car . . . probably three times. I finally figured out what she was saying: 'I didn't do it.' Go figure. I think she was just majorly delirious. Gotta run. Ski-ya later."

Jodi put the phone in her purse.

Kat was alive. There was still a chance she'd make it. Jodi whispered, *Thank you, Jesus.* More than anything, Jodi wanted to see Kat for herself—right then. But Bruce had said visiting hours were over. She considered chancing a visit anyway. Then again, without a car, and with limited cash for taxis, she resolved herself to visit Kat in the morning instead.

At the same time, she was puzzled by what Bruce had said that Kat had mumbled.

Kat "didn't do" what?

Jodi was considering several options when a new idea hit her like a ton of bricks. Maybe Kat was claiming she didn't give the drugs to the boy who had died. If she had, that would make Kat an accessory to murder. What's more, Jodi and Bruce had witnessed the scene, so they could be called to testify against her.

Was that it?

Bruce arrived at work fifteen minutes before his shift. His eyes were red and slightly puffy from a restless, fitful sleep. Thoughts from last evening had plagued him throughout the night: If the syringe from the dead boy came from their clinic, how would the guy have come into possession of it? Did he steal it? That was one possibility—but not a good one.

He knew the clinic had an alarm system. He also figured as an employee he would have been informed had there been a break-in. So, how did the guy get ahold of it? And, what was in the syringe that killed him?

Then again, Bruce was perfectly willing to admit that, as Jodi had suggested, he could be all wrong. Maybe the syringe wasn't from the Pet Vet supply. To satisfy his curiosity, and knowing full well that Saturdays were ultra busy, he arrived early for work.

The supply room containing cases of the unused syringes was located on the main floor. Bruce found it open, as was typically the case at this time of day. He stepped inside, located a brown cardboard box marked Ace Medical Systems Syringes on the third shelf. He withdrew a sealed, individual sample of the unopened product.

One side of the sterile wrapper was transparent, the other side a white paper with green type. The contents were described as a 3ml 21G1 Luer-Lok™ Latex Free syringe. Bruce compared it to the syringe he had taken from the boy last night. It was an exact match. Same red plunger. Same reference number. Same lot number.

Out of concern that their facility may have been compromised,

Bruce knew he had to inform Dr. Blackstone. He placed the unused syringe in the box and returned the box to the third shelf. Behind him he heard footsteps.

"May I inquire what you are doing, Bruce?"

Bruce spun around, surprised to see his boss in the doorway. "Oh, hi, Dr. Blackstone. Actually, there's something I was about to come and see you about."

"Yes, and what might that be? I haven't much time this morning. Be quick with it." Dr. Blackstone folded his left arm over his right. This kept his watch in plain view. Bruce observed a few bloodstains on Dr. Blackstone's white lab jacket. Not unusual since animal surgery was part of the scope of their work at the clinic.

"Well, last night my friend and I went to . . . to this rave. That's um, like, a dance party." Bruce, unsure whether Dr. Blackstone would know what a rave was, started to explain further. "See, there's a DJ, and kids from all over—"

"What you do with your free time is no concern of mine."

"Um, right. But see, I found this." Bruce pulled the syringe from last night out of his pocket. He fumbled for a long moment to unwrap it. As he worked, he heard Dr. Blackstone exhale a puff of impatient air.

"Well . . . you see . . . sir, it looked a whole lot like one of ours, which didn't make sense."

"I agree. And I'm sorry to cut you off, but—"

"If I can just say . . . I compared it this morning to one of those." Bruce pointed to the box on the shelf. "And, like, it matches perfectly. And so, what I can't figure for the life of me is how some kid ends up with one, you know?"

Dr. Blackstone leaned his head to one side. "May I see the syringe you're holding?" His fingers beckoned with a rapid twitch.

"Sure thing." Bruce handed it over. "See, what bothers me is that we only use these syringes to tranquilize the animals with a ketamine solution before surgery, right?"

Dr. Blackstone held the syringe up to the light. "That's correct."

Bruce offered, "There's still some solution, or whatever, left in it. Plus, you know how we've been making batches of the ketamine-filled syringes for other clinics? I wonder if this is somehow one of them. I . . . I figured you might be able to analyze what's inside."

Dr. Blackstone lowered the syringe and placed it in his lab coat pocket. "That's certainly within the realm of possibility—that is *if* I can find the time. Speaking of time, I've got a tight schedule this morning." He turned to leave.

"Ah . . . there's one more thing." Bruce hesitated to detain him further.

Dr. Blackstone turned halfway around, one hand lingering on the doorjamb. "And that would be?"

"Well, we found it next to the body of a dead boy."

Dr. Blackstone raised an eyebrow. His forehead wrinkled as if his mind was lost in a deep mystery. The intense look in his eyes made Bruce uncomfortable. Maybe he shouldn't have said anything. After all, there was probably nothing to it.

"Bruce, you did the right thing . . . bringing this to my attention." Dr. Blackstone stepped back into the supply room next to Bruce and then nodded toward the hallway. "This is serious, indeed. I'd like to have a word with you in my office." He placed his hand in the small of Bruce's back to give him a friendly nudge.

Bruce followed him down the hall and then into the office.

"Please, sit down." Dr. Blackstone motioned to a chair facing his desk. He leaned against the edge of the credenza and folded his arms.

"That's quite a collection of spiders, Dr. Blackstone." Bruce eyed the terrarium behind his boss. "Funny, I didn't know they could live together like that, you know, all three in the same cage."

Dr. Blackstone cleared his throat. "I guess when you know your place, nobody has to get hurt, now do they?" His thick eyebrows narrowed, the right side arching as he spoke.

"Um, you can say that again." Bruce swallowed.

"Now, as you can imagine, I'm troubled at the news of these

missing syringes. Naturally, if someone has stolen ketamine from this or any other clinic, I want to do everything in my power to find the culprit and bring him to justice."

Bruce was relieved. "I thought you'd be concerned—"

"That's an understatement. Bruce, you've been with us, what, three or four months?"

"About that, yes, sir."

"Then you'd know that when properly administered in the prescribed dosage ketamine disassociates the nervous system from the mind. And that's what makes it such a tempting choice for drug addicts."

Bruce scratched his head. "I don't follow. How would that be, like, interesting to a druggie?"

"In short, ketamine is a powerful substance that produces an out-of-body experience that can last several hours. Mind you, it's not designed for human consumption. But when a human takes it, usually mixed with valium, they sustain the sensation of floating above their body."

"Wow. Really?"

"That's why it's illegal to sell it over the counter in every state. Only a certified vet may purchase it. But when it hits the streets, my understanding is that kids call it Special K."

Bruce sat up straight in his chair. Where had he heard that name before? Wasn't it at the rave?

"You'll never believe this, Dr. Blackstone, but just last night I was approached by a guy who asked me if I'd like Special K! Gee, I had no idea."

"Here's the catch." Dr. Blackstone pulled his chair away from his desk, sat down, and folded his hands as if about to launch into a lecture on the subject. "Ketamine is a seizuregenic drug. True, we use it ten, maybe fifteen times a day in this clinic. But in the hands of an untrained individual, that person is literally playing with death. That's why we're required by law to keep all ketamine supplies under lock and key."

Bruce's mind drifted to Kat. *So that's what happened to her,* he thought. *She must have taken the drug and gone into a seizure. Ditto for the boy, only it killed him.*

"Tell me, Bruce, where was the location of this dance party?"

"The rave? Oh, it was downtown Philly, on, um, Christopher Columbus Boulevard . . . in an old warehouse. Can't say exactly. It was late, and dark—"

"Not to worry." Dr. Blackstone leaned forward, the palms of his hands resting on the surface in front of him. "But I am wondering, Bruce. You've said 'we' several times. Is there anybody else that can support your claim about the death of the boy . . . from what might have been one of our syringes?"

Bruce was thankful that his boss was taking this seriously. "Yes, actually. My friend Jodi saw him, too."

"Jodi. And her last name?"

"Adams. Jodi Adams. She goes to my school. She even took a picture of him."

Dr. Blackstone's eyes widened. For an instant, Bruce thought his boss appeared panicked. Who wouldn't be, especially if something from their lab was involved in a death.

"Listen, Bruce. I'd like to speak with this friend of yours. Could you arrange for her to stop by . . . say, later today?"

"I'll sure try."

"You do that—I'm counting on you. This is of utmost importance." His intercom crackled.

"Doctor?" The voice from the speakerphone filled the room.

"Yes?"

"Your 8:30 surgery is prepped and ready."

"Thank you, Susan." Dr. Blackstone punched a button on the phone and then stood to leave. "Naturally, I'd make room in my schedule whenever a meeting with your friend, Miss Jodi Adams, can be arranged. Now, if you'll excuse me."

n retrospect, Jodi wasn't surprised to be the only person at Kat's hospital bedside. She knew Kat's dad was doing time in a New Jersey jail, while her mother, a borderline alcoholic and drug user, was in a jail of her own making. "A free spirit," was the way Kat had described her mom before the first time Jodi met her. That was an understatement.

Presently, Jodi sat in an uncomfortable, low-back chair. She had pulled it close to Kat's side, positioning it so that she could occasionally dab Kat's forehead with a cool, damp washcloth. Kat remained motionless, a white sheet pulled up to her chest, the bed slightly elevated underneath her head. The only sound in the room came from the chorus of *beeps* and *chirps* emitted by an assortment of equipment adjacent to the headboard.

It took all the restraint Jodi could muster to keep from running out of the building. She hated hospitals. Always had, ever since the death of her grandfather. The smells nauseated her. She could handle the dentist's office just fine. But hospitals, with their rows of rooms filled with sickness, suffering, and the constant parade of nameless doctors and nurses armed with clipboards and needles, unsettled her.

She yawned, covering her mouth as she did. Naturally, it didn't help that she was exhausted from the night before. She had arrived an hour earlier, having first stopped by the InstyFoto Mart to drop off the disposable camera for developing. She'd pick up the pictures from the rave later that morning.

Upon Jodi's arrival, the nurse explained that speaking to Kat in low tones was good therapy, but not to expect a response. Kat was heavily medicated to prevent another seizure. She drifted in and out of consciousness, although she'd been unconscious all morning. Jodi learned that Kat's blood work was being processed at the lab and they'd know the results in twenty-four hours. Meanwhile, it was a waiting game.

Jodi crossed her legs and then hooked her hair over her right ear. A painful mixture of emotions, like a fountain, sprang up inside her as she watched Kat lying unconscious. Jodi leaned forward and, with a soft squeeze of Kat's hand, continued to vocalize her feelings.

"Kat, I . . . I thought you were, like, finally coming to understand God, you know? You asked me all those great questions and, um, you pushed me for real answers. It's funny how you even made me rethink stuff I've always known but taken for granted. You started to believe life was worth living, remember? And things began to, like, make sense as you learned more about God. You said so yourself."

Jodi gently dabbed Kat's forehead again. A thin, clear oxygen tube strapped beneath her nostrils provided a steady, regulated supply of purified air. She was careful not to dislodge it.

"So what happened, Kat? What were you thinking? How could you do such a foolish thing? I mean, to gamble with your life? Maybe it was all me . . . maybe I was too pushy, too anxious to see you invite Jesus into your heart. I don't know. Did I come on too strong? Or, was I too laid-back? Too afraid to let you know what I was really thinking?"

Jodi folded her hands in her lap. In this unguarded moment, Jodi thought Kat looked bad. Real bad. The IV drip bag hung in midair, suspended by a cold, stainless-steel pole. The supply line was taped in place on Kat's arm where it entered a vein.

"Kat, I want you to know that, um, I love you . . . like the sister I never had. Hard to believe, huh? I mean, we're, like, as different as they come. That doesn't matter to me. You've got to make it . . . you just have to."

Jodi wiped the tears from her eyes with the back of her hand.

"I know you can hear me, Kat."

She crossed her arms, looked out the window, then back at her friend.

"You know what else? This is so, like, unfair to me . . . to us. What gave you the right to give up on life? I've made a pretty serious investment in you, Kat. I believe in you. You know why? Because—surprise—God gave me a love for you, girlfriend. I would never have thought that was possible."

Jodi tilted her head to one side as a fresh memory surfaced. "Do you remember what you said the day we first met? I'll never forget it. You said, 'Hey, it's me and the Christian . . . your God must have a sense of humor.'"

She sat back in her chair. A lone tear rolled down her cheek at the recollection. She took a deep, slow breath, trying to regain her composure. For several minutes, her gaze remained fixed on Kat's pale white face.

Kat's eyes fluttered open. Jodi had to blink to make sure she wasn't imagining it. Kat managed to roll her head in Jodi's direction.

"Hey there, sleeping beauty," Jodi said, offering a warm smile. "You're doing just great, girl." She thought Kat was about to say something. Jodi placed her forefinger to her lips. "Shh. You don't have to say anything. Save your strength, Kat. Whatever it is, it can wait."

Kat's head flopped slowly side to side.

"I didn't . . . do . . . it . . ."

Jodi weighed her next few words before speaking. "Let me say that I think I know what you mean and, um, I believe you—you didn't have anything to do with that boy dying. Honest, I believe you weren't involved."

Kat's face tightened. She lifted her neck and head off the pillow for a weak second before plopping back down. "No . . . I, I didn't . . ." She closed her eyes, evidently too tired to finish her sentence.

"Wait a second," Jodi said. She picked up the Styrofoam cup filled with crushed ice and a plastic spoon from the roll-around table. "Here, try to suck on a little of this ice, okay? The nurse said it will help your throat feel better."

Jodi raised a spoonful to Kat's dry lips. Kat managed to ingest a few meager ice shavings.

"Are you saying you didn't take the drugs? Is that what you mean?"

Kat reopened her eyes. Jodi detected an affirmative nod, although still weak. "Yes."

"Listen, Kat. I want to believe you. Really I do." Jodi set the cup and spoon to the side after supplying another serving. "I don't know how to say this. But, like, I saw the needle you used and, well, it was empty."

Kat licked her lips as she shook her head in disagreement.

Holding Kat's hand as she spoke, Jodi offered a helpless shrug and said, "What you're saying, I mean, it just doesn't make sense. And guess what? I'm going to give the doctor the needle so they can figure out what's causing all this freaky stuff with your body."

Kat closed her eyes and slipped back into an unconscious state. Jodi felt her hand go limp.

She lowered her voice. "I'm leaving now, but I'll be back real soon. See, I've got to, like, find out who sold this junk that almost killed you . . . and killed that boy. And I have a strong hunch where to start looking."

* * *

Jodi paid the fee for parking in the hospital's multilevel garage and then headed north onto Old York Road. She was driving her family's Mazda 626. Her dad called it the "Plain Jane" mobile, because the little white sedan certainly wouldn't turn any heads or set any speed records, but the four-door, four-cylinder was super-reliable basic transportation. Best of all, her dad paid the insurance.

At the first red light, she remembered to turn her cell phone back on. She had been required to switch it off while inside the hospital.

Traffic was sparse, and she figured she could make the InstyFoto Mart over in Huntingdon Valley in ten minutes; twelve if she hit the forever red at Old York and Old Welsh Roads.

As she drove, her thoughts drifted back to something she had read in Ephesians 5 during her personal devotions the night before. And while she had read the entire chapter, verse 11 came to mind: *Have nothing to do with the fruitless deeds of darkness, but rather expose them.*

Given her current situation, those words struck her as being more than mere coincidence. God was speaking to her through the Scriptures; she felt compelled to learn the truth about the dead boy and Kat.

After the fiasco with Officer Dexter, she was tempted to let it go, just as Bruce had suggested in the first place. Kat was in the hospital getting the care she needed. Wasn't that all that mattered? Why should she care about the boy, a complete stranger she never knew? Why should she spend a beautiful Saturday afternoon trying to make sense out of last night's hellhole?

Her phone jumped to life on the seat next to her with a simple series of *beep*s. As someone who enjoyed classical music, she detested the gimmicky melody settings. She thought it ironic that the only "classical" music most Americans would ever hear was the annoying, electronic renditions of Bach and Beethoven popularized by cell phones.

She snatched it up after one ring.

"Hello?"

"Jodi. It's Bruce."

"Hey, how's it going? Get any sleep?"

"Me? Not much. Where are you?"

"I'm on Old York . . . just passing McDonald's. Just finished seeing Kat. Oh, and she, like, woke up for a minute. That's a good sign, I guess."

"Sure is. Hey, I've got just a minute—"

"Yeah, I forgot you're a big-time vet." She laughed.

"Nice. Anyway, remember how last night I said I thought that syringe looked kinda familiar? Like it might be one of ours?"

"Uh-huh."

"It matched."

"Really? Wow. Did you talk to your boss about it?"

"Actually, yes. He was real concerned, too, you know, worried that someone might have been hurt by the misuse of it."

"So you told him about the boy *and* Kat?"

There was a moment of silence.

"Bruce?"

"I'm here. You know, I forgot to mention Kat. But I did tell him about the corpse—"

"You have such a way with words."

"Anyway, listen. He'd like to talk to you—"

"Me? Why me?"

"Only because I mentioned that we both were there and we both, like, saw the same thing. He just wants to ask you a few questions before he files a report with the police, or whatever. Should take fifteen minutes, max."

"So, like, when should I see him?"

"Can you come now?"

Jodi thought for a moment. "Yeah, I guess. I was going to stop and pick up my film, but that can wait until afterward."

"Cool. I'll tell him you're on the way. I'll be working all day so give me a shout when you stop by."

"Wait a minute. Do I *have* to admit I know you?" Jodi said.

"As long as I don't have to admit I know you, either," he said with a laugh.

Carlos Martinez checked his rearview mirror. The black, hopped-up Suburban was still behind him. At first he dismissed its presence as a fluke. But five turns later, with the beastly looking SUV still dogging his tail, his thoughts raced over the possibilities.

He didn't know anybody who owned a vehicle like it; the Huntingdon Valley police didn't use such transportation; he doubted it was the FBI; and this wasn't a case of road rage, of that he was sure. He hadn't cut anybody off. Quite the contrary. He had been driving slower, thanks to a crushed, heavily bandaged finger.

Carlos tried to ignore whoever it was. He had bigger problems at the moment, thank you very much. Like, where to find $7,000 to pay back the Russians. He had spent every last dollar on jewelry, clothes, and stereo equipment. There was no way he could scrape that much cash together. Certainly not by the noon deadline, which loomed on the horizon less than forty-five minutes away.

His busted finger throbbed at the thought.

Instead, Carlos was headed for the Pet Vet Wellness Center to see Reverend Bud. He had arranged the meeting figuring it was better to come clean with what he had done than to deal with two Russian barbarians. He was fairly certain Reverend Bud would cut him some slack. Even call off the Russian dogs. Or at least maybe loan him the money to keep Illya and Zhenya out of his hair.

Carlos had plenty of time as he drove to rehearse his story. Satisfied, he figured it would push all the right buttons: His sister, a lesbian, had contracted AIDS and couldn't afford the medication. Without it, she'd die. Her health insurance, a giant HMO provider, wouldn't cover the cost of her prescriptions. His parents had disowned her for her sexual choice. He was her only chance. How could he let down his sister?

He skimmed the drug money to help her out. Who wouldn't?

At least that was his story.

There was one problem. It was a complete fabrication. All, except the part about his lesbian sister. That much was true. As for the rest of the story, he'd do his best to sound convincing.

Carlos slowed to a stop at a light on Old Welsh Road, a two-lane, windy strip of asphalt divided by a double yellow line. The Suburban, at least the last few times he stopped at a light, had hung back from him. This time, however, it pulled up on his tail; the bumper-mounted winch, so enormous it could double as a cattle prod on the front of a train, towered above the back of his little two-door hatchback.

His heart zoomed within his chest. He was tempted to turn around to face this clown, but he didn't want to appear anxious. He settled for a prolonged look in his side mirror. He noticed the windows were tinted with a dark, reflective material that prevented him from seeing inside. Even the windshield was tinted. As Carlos knew all too well, having considered doing the same himself, tinting the windshield was illegal in Pennsylvania.

The light turned green.

Carlos stepped on the accelerator but got an added boost from the Suburban. The joker had actually bumped into his car. A blast of adrenaline raced through his nervous system. He swore and then stomped on the gas; not that his four-cylinder was capable of outrunning the Suburban. At least the Suburban was physically off his tail—for the moment.

Now what? He'd call 911, but his cell phone had been knocked onto the floor and slipped under the passenger seat from the impact.

He leaned over and, trying to keep his eyes on the road, frantically felt around for it with his hand. But the phone, his lifeline, remained out of reach. He sat upright, both hands on the steering wheel.

He glanced at his rearview mirror and swore again. *Those morons are gonna ram me*, he thought. He braced himself and mentally urged the car to go faster, even though it was already pushed to the max. The palms of his hands sweated as he gripped the wheel.

Just before impact, the Suburban swerved instead and pulled alongside him, traveling in the lane of oncoming traffic. A block ahead, Carlos was fast approaching another red light. He slammed on the brakes to avoid running through a busy intersection. His nearly bald tires screeched for dear life. The Suburban slowed, too, and remained on his left.

Carlos stole another look and saw that it was equipped with a complete off-road package. Oversize nubby tires. Tubular running boards. Chrome mud flaps. Thick leap springs. Even as the diesel engine idled next to him, it snorted like a provoked rhinoceros waiting to stampede.

The tinted passenger side window lowered.

Zhenya, the Russian, stared at him through dark sunglasses.

"Pull over, punk." Zhenya spit the words, and then flicked a cigarette butt in Carlos's direction.

No way, Carlos thought. *And lose another finger?*

A rush of fear overwhelmed him. The hair on the back of his neck bristled. Why were they chasing him? It wasn't noon yet. Were they afraid he might skip town? Right, and go where? His chest tightened; his heart felt as if it might suddenly implode. He'd never make it to the vet clinic.

He had to buy some time, but nobody was selling.

Then an unexpected idea struck him. He knew these roads; they probably didn't. Up ahead, using the topography to his advantage, he'd try to shake them. A long shot, true. But as a drowning man he wasn't about to reject the only option in sight.

"Look . . . I've got, um, the cash," he said, his voice shaking. "For real . . . Just, like, follow me, okay? I'll . . . I'll take you to it."

Zhenya turned to confer with Illya, who sat behind the wheel of the beast. Zhenya looked back at Carlos, this time over the top of his sunglasses. "No tricks." He jabbed at the air, signaling Carlos to pull ahead.

Carlos hesitated long enough for the light to turn green, then lurched forward. His eyes darted between the road ahead and the Suburban behind. He took a rapid series of short breaths to clear his head. He had one chance to make his move.

One last card to play.

If it didn't work—well, it just had to.

He knew in a few minutes Old Welsh Road would bend sharply to the left, followed by a series of tight S-curves, like that of a corkscrew. He was also counting on the heavily tree-lined road that obstructed the view of Paper Mill Road intersecting from the left. At the last possible second, he planned to dart off Old Welsh Road onto the rarely traveled Paper Mill Road. If all went as planned, he'd make the turn and the Russians wouldn't have time to react. After that he'd have to wing it.

Once on Paper Mill Road he might have sixty seconds, maybe ninety, to lose them.

Another look in the mirror. Illya and Zhenya were an ideal distance behind, Carlos thought. Not that he'd ever been in a situation such as this to know for certain. It was just a gut feeling.

On his right, he whipped past a minimart, a gas station, a school, and then a church. Ironically, the thought to pray crossed his mind, but he dismissed it. He figured he didn't believe in prayer, so why start now? Besides, he'd always thought it was stupid the way people in trouble would try to bargain with God, like, "God, if you get me out of this . . . I'll do anything." No, he wasn't about to go soft.

Twenty seconds more and they'd engage the bend. Rather than slow, he accelerated. As he entered the curve, his car leaned hard to the right as he banked to the left. His tires squealed at the abuse. He yanked the wheel in the opposite direction, momentarily crossing the center yellow line, and then reversed the move to navigate the S-curves.

Behind him he watched as the Suburban hardly broke a sweat at the rapid shifts in the road.

It was now or never. He knew the Paper Mill cutoff was just around the next cluster of trees. He raced his engine for all it was worth, briefly widening the distance between himself and the Russians. They, in turn, hustled to catch up like a charging bull, black diesel soot pouring out of their side exhaust pipes.

At the last second, Carlos slammed on his brakes and jerked the wheel to the left with all his might, then immediately punched the gas pedal, cramming it to the floorboard. The car almost rolled.

Carlos made the turn. Within seconds he hit 59 miles per hour, although his heart was speeding along faster than that. The posted limit was 20.

He was almost too numb to see if Illya made the turn. But he had to know if the killers were still on his tail. He twisted around and, at the top of his lungs, shouted, "Woo-hoo! Take that, you Russian scumbags!" as his car rocketed across the bumpy country road.

They were nowhere in sight.

Carlos guessed they'd back up and pursue him. But at least he'd bought a little extra time—maybe enough to lose them.

He spun back around to focus on the path ahead of him a split second too late. A deer and her fawn were crossing the road dead ahead. Without thinking, he forced the wheel hard and to the left. The bald tires, having outlived their usefulness, sent the car into a spin. He struggled without success to maintain control.

Although Carlos missed the deer, his car careened over the side of an ivy-covered, steep embankment as if pulled downward by an unstoppable magnetic force. His stomach jumped up into his throat.

He pounced on the brake pedal with both feet.

Nothing. The brake lines must have been severed when he went over the edge. Bounding down the hillside, his car rocked back and forth like a little metal ball in the hands of a pinball wizard. Each jolt knocked out what little breath he managed to gulp.

"No-o-o-o!"

Carlos plowed helplessly through the tall grass and into a three-rail wooden fence. The windshield instantly shattered into a thousand pieces just as Carlos, on reflex, released the wheel and raised both hands to prevent the shards of glass from spraying him in the face.

"Oh God, oh God, oh God!!"

The car continued to pitch down the hill with the speed of a runaway train. It didn't stop until it slammed into the base of a walnut tree. The hood crumpled like an accordion; the front end pulverized beyond repair.

Carlos blacked out on impact.

Hi, I'm here to see Dr. Blackstone." Jodi stood at the receptionist's window, hands at her side. Her purse hung neatly over her right shoulder. She read the woman's nametag: Tina Linda.

"Do you have an appointment?" Tina asked, consulting her appointment book with a frown.

"Yes, sort of. I believe he's expecting me."

"And whom may I say is here?"

"Jodi Adams. I'm a friend of Bruce Arnold," Jodi offered, as if his name would help.

"Oh, you know Bruce? Nice guy. In fact, you just missed him."

"Really? I thought he was working today."

"Yeah—was. Boss gave him the rest of the day off. Lucky guy, especially with the weather being so nice and all. Excuse me while I see if Dr. Blackstone is available. Feel free to have a seat." Tina motioned to the lobby waiting area and then picked up the phone.

That was odd, Jodi thought as she sat on the edge of a chair by the fishtank. *I just spoke with Bruce minutes ago. He didn't say anything about cutting out early. What's up with that? So, like, I'm gonna have this meeting . . . alone?* Lost in thought, her eyes followed an orange swordfish. It darted into a hole in the side of a sunken ship. The ship, surrounded by wispy-looking brown kelp, rested on the pebbled bottom of the fishtank.

"Miss Adams?"

Jodi looked up. Her eyes narrowed briefly. Dr. Blackstone, she assumed. He held the door to the inner hallway open as he examined the waiting area.

"Yes, I'm Jodi Adams," she said. She ran her fingers through her hair and then rose from her chair.

"If you'll follow me."

She offered a tentative smile. "Um, sure thing."

Dr. Blackstone walked briskly down the hall, his white lab coat flowing in his wake. On both her left and right was a row of doors. Some closed, some open. She could hear dogs barking and birds squawking behind those that were closed.

As she passed room 5, she glanced inside. It had a stainless-steel examination table, a small sink, a medicine cabinet, and a chair. Pretty much what she'd expected.

At the end of the hall, she turned left and followed Dr. Blackstone to a room marked "Restricted Area—Authorized Personnel Only." She watched him enter a code on the electronic, wall-mounted keypad.

"I appreciate your coming, and on such short notice," he said over his shoulder. "Things are rather crazy in this wing. We can talk more comfortably in here." With a sharp *click,* the door lock released.

Inside, she noted, was an impressive surgical suite, as nice as the one she had experienced at Abington Hospital's state-of-the-art facility. She was drawn to a bank of large windows that overlooked a berm of tall pine trees.

"I designed the facility to maximize the view," Dr. Blackstone said, his arms folded. "When you spend hours cutting animals open, as I do, the picturesque scenery renews the mind." He spoke the words in a detached, clinical tone.

He continued. "What you don't see, Jodi, is the extensive sound-proofing. Nothing that happens in this room can be heard outside these walls. If you'd like to test it out, be my guest and yell."

Jodi turned from the view toward Dr. Blackstone, clutching her purse to her side. She felt chilled. Why would he say something like that? She definitely didn't like the feeling of isolation that swept over her, or the way Dr. Blackstone studied her. She couldn't shake the feeling that he wasn't trustworthy.

He forced a smile. "Naturally, the soundproofing is for the benefit of my clients in the other parts of the building. It prevents them from unnecessary discomfort when we're in surgery." He stroked his goatee. "You know, the sounds from drilling or sawing can be unsettling for some visitors."

"Thanks for the, um, tour." Jodi was ready to get this over with as fast as possible. "So, like, Bruce said you wanted to see me . . . about last night or something."

"Indeed. I understand that you both had quite the adventure at that rave."

Jodi nodded. "That's an understatement, I guess." They had met less than a handful of minutes ago and yet she sensed there was something dark about him. But what? The shifting in his eyes? The stiffness of his movements? Then again, maybe she was just over-reacting from lack of a good night's sleep.

"As you can imagine, I have a few questions. Bruce thought you might be able to shed some light on things. Let's have a seat in my office. I promise I'll only keep you long enough to finish our business." He pointed to a door to her right.

Jodi walked to the opening, peered through the doorway, stepped in, and took a seat at his direction. She couldn't help but see the terrarium with its assortment of spiders. She held herself and shuddered as she watched their movements.

"Is it too cool in here?" Dr. Blackstone asked.

She shook her head. "No. I just hate spiders—they give me the creeps. Sorry, no offense."

"That's a completely understandable reaction," Dr. Blackstone said with a taut smile. Still standing, he added, "Forgive my manners. May I provide you something to drink? A Coke? Fruit juice? Water?"

"Water would be fine, thank you." She relaxed a little, appreciating his offer of hospitality. Maybe he wasn't such a cold fish after all.

Dr. Blackstone pulled two paper cups from the dispenser attached to the five-gallon water cooler, filled each, and stepped momentarily out of the office. A second later, he returned with the drink cups and two paper napkins.

"Here you go." He handed her a cup and a napkin.

"Thank you." Jodi took the cup and sipped it. She was more thirsty than she realized. She drank some more. Finished, she dabbed her mouth with the napkin and then balanced the cup on the edge of the armrest.

"I'll get to the point. Bruce gave me this," Dr. Blackstone said. He leaned against the edge of his desk and withdrew the syringe from his lab jacket. "Do you recognize it?"

She identified it immediately. "Sure thing. Bruce and I found that, like, right beside him."

"Who?"

"Actually, I can't say for sure. That's something I'm working to figure out." Jodi bit her lip. She hadn't planned to reveal that piece of information. "I mean, he was, like, seventeen or so. We think he died from an overdose of whatever was in there."

"So you're saying this person died?"

"Well, that's what we *think*—see, Bruce felt for a pulse but couldn't find one." Jodi fought an overwhelming urge to yawn. She covered her mouth.

He leaned forward. "Did you alert the police?"

"As a matter of fact, I did." Jodi noticed his right eye twitch at that bit of information.

"What happened next? Did you and Bruce file a report?"

"Yes and no. See, the deal was, Bruce was taking our friend to the hospital, so he dropped me off at the police station." Jodi fidgeted with an earring. A small voice inside warned, *Don't say too much.* "Um, they—the police—didn't seem to be, like, too concerned about the drugs. They said they didn't have enough manpower or whatever." Jodi crossed her legs and was tempted to lean her head back against the wall behind her and close her eyes.

"When I told them about that body . . . they, um . . . they, I mean, *that* got their attention." She felt so tired, so incredibly woozy. What was happening? "I'm sorry, where was I?"

"The police report—"

"Oh, yeah." Jodi worked to recall the events. "So I take them to . . . to the rave and, gee, the body was, like, gone. No body, no crime, right?" Another deep yawn.

Dr. Blackstone folded his hands. "And what about this friend—"

"Kat Koffman."

"Was she somehow mixed up in all of this?"

"You could, um, say so. That's how everything started, you know? We went to find her and when we did, we found the dead boy, and . . . oh, yeah . . . and she had a needle, too."

"Is that so? Do you have it with you? May I see it, Jodi?" His tongue licked the bottom of his top lip like a hungry man waiting to be served dinner. She thought he was about to drool.

"Well, actually, yes, but . . . I'd like to keep it. You see, Kat's in the hospital . . . I, um, found her with it at the rave, like I said. Anyway, I was supposed to give it to . . . the doctor for some tests." Then, under her breath, she said, "Gee, I can't believe I forgot to do that."

She looked back at Dr. Blackstone and said, "Besides, it looks just like the one you're holding." She smiled. Seconds later, she felt her forehead with the back of her hand. "Excuse me. I . . . I'm feeling a little lightheaded." Her eyelids, heavy with sleep, closed. With a jolt, she jerked awake in time to hear Dr. Blackstone speak.

"I'm sorry to hear that," he said. His face remained stoic, impervious to her condition. "Just a few more questions."

Right now, all she needed was a pillow. Her eyes closed again. This time they didn't reopen.

* * *

Dr. Blackstone carried Jodi's limp body to the operating table. He strapped her legs and arms in place. He returned to his office, picked up her purse, and sat at his desk. He opened it and found the syringe almost immediately. His eyes widened in delight; one less piece of incriminating evidence. He removed the syringe and placed it in his center desk drawer.

With anticipation, like that of a thirsty man in the desert dying for a drink, he dumped the rest of the contents on his desk. A compact. Car keys. Assorted receipts. A few dollars. Several business cards. Driver's license. And the winning ticket to his personal lottery: a numbered claim check from the InstyFoto Mart.

A wide smile crossed his face.

He picked up the phone to dial Reverend Bud. While he waited for an answer, he carefully placed the items back into her purse. Minus one claim check.

Reverend Bud answered on the third ring.

"Yo, yo, whassup?"

Dr. Blackstone barked, "It's me. Where are you?"

"Whew. Dr. B., you've really gotta chill out, man. Like, wow, dude. I'm having serious trouble with your negative energy—"

"That's not the only problem you'll have, *dude*." Dr. Blackstone pounded the desk with his fist. "Now answer me. I don't have a second to waste."

"You know what? I hear the YMCA has these, like, really cool anger-management classes, see what I'm saying? Oh, and by the way, I'm on my way to the mother ship."

"You high again?" Dr. Blackstone knew better than to ask. It was as much an insult as a rhetorical question.

"Like a kite. But not too high to count to three. That's your donor count—"

"Careful. Not on the phone." Dr. Blackstone thought Reverend

Bud sounded especially wired and wasn't sure how much to risk talking by phone. Long ago, they'd worked out an arrangement of doublespeak that wouldn't tip their hand should the authorities monitor a cell phone transmission.

Dr. Blackstone was in a tight spot. He estimated that the gamma hydroxybutyric acid, or GHB, a knockout drug he had slipped into Jodi's water, would last only a few minutes more. He needed to clarify several details before she regained consciousness. If only Reverend Bud wouldn't compromise their secrets.

"I have with me a young lady who is, shall we say, indisposed. I believe you may have had a conversation with her last night. She was snooping around your dance party. Worse, she went so far as to alert those two jokers, Officer 'D' and—"

"That would be the good Sergeant—"

"Remember, no names. How solid is our financial arrangement with them?" Dr. Blackstone cradled the phone against his left ear with his shoulder.

"Dude, I'm spreading the grease nice and thick. We're talking super-sizing their usual order, you dig me?"

"Good. Did the pigs see anything, uh, let's say, unusual?"

"You know, I really don't feel loved, Dr. B. I mean, how about a little credit. The place was Ajax clean, know what I mean? Copperfield couldn't have made people disappear any faster."

Dr. Blackstone tapped his finger on the desk. "So where's the—"

"On ice," Reverend Bud said. "Yeah, he's in back chillin' with friends, you know what I'm saying?"

"Good. When can I expect this delivery?" Dr. Blackstone consulted his watch and then drummed his fingers on the desk.

"I kinda got the munchies. Figure I'll grab some USDA-inspected pressed meat on a bun . . . you know, America's favorite health food. Um, so maybe thirty minutes. Is that cool, Bossman?"

Dr. Blackstone rubbed his eyes. "That'll work. Not a minute more. I'm alerting the others as soon as we hang up—so don't make us wait."

"Hey, so whatcha gonna do with the girl?"

Dr. Blackstone was surprised by the question. Reverend Bud usually didn't ask about such details. He cleared his throat. "She's nosy. She needs to be taught a lesson. What's it to you?"

"Nothing, but dude, is that, like, necessary?"

"That's not your business. She knows too much—or thinks she does. She even took a picture of a certain missing person. I will not have our entire operation jeopardized by some do-gooder. And you, of all people, should know I don't tolerate loose ends."

"Well, my vote would be—"

"You don't have a vote," Dr. Blackstone snapped. "I'll detain her until my secretary pays a visit to the InstyFoto Mart, if you must know. Jodi's 'Kodak moments' are as good as shredded. In the meantime, that pesky troublemaker is going to learn a few new things about spiders."

Dr. Blackstone craned his neck to one side and looked through the doorway at Jodi. She was starting to wake up. He lowered his voice and spoke through clenched teeth, "Now don't make me wait for my delivery."

He slammed down the phone.

The black Suburban skidded to an angry stop at the edge of Paper Mill Road, spraying gravel and dust in every direction. Illya and Zhenya jumped out. The two men walked to the front of their vehicle and met by the hood. Their feet were planted at the precise spot where Carlos had spun out of control.

Neither man spoke.

The Huntingdon Valley Golf Course, with its rolling fairways and manicured greens, filled the valley below them. Illya squinted in the midday sun and noted that Carlos had crashed into a tree at the edge of a putting green. Zhenya removed his sunglasses and lifted a pair of binoculars to his hazel-brown eyes. A freshly lit, unfiltered cigarette dangled from his dry lips.

Illya broke the silence. "Say me what you think?"

Zhenya's nostrils flared as a puff of smoke, like fire from the nose of a dragon, was expelled. "I think he dead."

Illya reached into his suit coat pocket. He pulled out a handful of sunflower seeds and popped one in his mouth as he weighed the options. He spit the shell on the ground. "I say we make sure."

"*Da.*" Zhenya lowered the field glasses with a nod.

"Come," said Illya, who spit another shell onto the ground. A dark patch of clouds passed overhead, momentarily blocking the sunlight. The men took their places inside the SUV, Illya behind the wheel, Zhenya riding shotgun.

Illya mashed a button marked 4x4 LOW with his forefinger, and then plowed down the hillside with the power of a bulldozer on steroids. He followed the pathway through the fence blazed by the not-so-fortunate Carlos. They reached the wreckage inside ninety seconds.

Illya parked the Suburban twenty feet away. He stepped out of the vehicle without bothering to close the door and then snaked his way through the underbrush, careful not to dirty his alligator-skin shoes. Illya stopped alongside the hatchback and glanced inside at the front seat. He reached in. His fingers lingered on the side of Carlos's neck. He took three steps back and then turned toward the Suburban.

Illya looked at Zhenya. "He should no have run."

"Played ball in wrong team," Zhenya said flatly. Zhenya stood by the rear of the SUV, his arms folded tightly. A lazy wisp of smoke rose from the end of his cigarette. He remained as emotionless as a guard in front of Buckingham Palace.

Illya said, "Light it up."

Having received his orders, Zhenya opened the rear tailgate, grabbed a red five-gallon plastic container and approached the hatchback. With a smooth, sweeping motion, he doused the entire car in gasoline. After draining the container, he tossed the empty receptacle through the busted windshield into the front seat next to Carlos. He walked over and stood next to Illya.

Zhenya, about to ignite the bonfire by flicking his cigarette on top of the newly baptized car, was stopped by Illya. "Not so fast, Comrade." Illya held up his hand as if directing traffic. "Remember, Carlos worth much. Bring him. We see good Dr. Blackstone next."

Zhenya dragged Carlos out of the car by the back of his collar, took a final drag from his cigarette, and then tossed it inside. Illya and Zhenya turned and walked toward the Suburban. Behind them, the car burst into flames. As they sped away, they could hear the gas tank explode.

Neither man looked back.

* * *

The room came slowly into focus as Jodi's eyes blinked open. Still disoriented, her mind tried to make sense of the emerging picture. Why was she lying down? What was preventing her from sitting up? Was this a hospital? Was she sick? She wished the fog in her head would clear.

"Where am I?" she said. A yawn escaped as she spoke the words.

"Ah, I see you have awakened," Dr. Blackstone said, standing at her side. "How was your nap?"

At the sound of his voice, she struggled to sit up again but quickly discovered that to try was pointless. Her arms and legs were strapped securely in place. Jodi turned her head and looked directly into Dr. Blackstone's inky black eyes.

He offered a thin smile in return. "I can tell by the look on your face that you were not expecting to be in this position."

"Let me go, this instant, or I promise I'll . . . I'll . . ."

"You'll what? Run to the police?" He folded his arms and placed a finger to his forehead. "And what story will you tell them this time?"

Her heart skipped a beat. *Me and my big mouth,* she thought. *Can't believe I told him about them.*

"Jodi, I'd much rather play a game. Do you like games?"

"That depends." *Where is he going with this?*

"Well, let's play anyway," Dr. Blackstone said with a mischievous wink. "And let's call our game 'Little Miss Muffet.' I'm sure you're familiar with the nursery rhyme."

Jodi shut her eyes and hoped that when she reopened them, she'd be anywhere but in his presence. Her eyes still closed, she heard Dr. Blackstone recite the words of the rhyme. *"Little Miss Muffet sat on a tuffet, eating her curds and whey. When along came a spider . . ."* He stopped before finishing.

Jodi opened her eyes in time to watch him disappear into his office. *This can't be happening,* she thought. *He wouldn't, would he?* As she waited, her cell phone jumped to life. Jodi twisted her neck in the direction of her purse, wishing she could somehow manage to reach over and answer it. *Whoever you are, I'm here! I need help!* She mouthed the words, hoping the caller would somehow magically receive her message.

The phone stopped ringing after four rings.

A minute later, Dr. Blackstone returned wearing rubber-looking gloves on his hands. He held something large and orange-colored. He began to speak as he approached the operating table.

"To begin our little game, Jodi, did you know there are more than thirty-five thousand known species of spiders? About eight hundred are true tarantulas. Take this one, for instance." He held out his hands near her face. "Meet Delilah. She's the Goliath Bird Eater you noticed in my office, the largest spider in the world, I might add. Pretty, isn't she?"

Jodi turned her head away.

"Humor me," Dr. Blackstone said. "If you look closely, you'll see she's got eight eyes on a small bump right there on the front of her body, just above the fangs. As you can guess, she's not your pet store variety spider."

Jodi closed her eyes. "What do you want?"

He ignored the question. "As a member of the American Tarantula Society, I've discovered I'm not the only person who enjoys owning such a unique pet. Thousands of other individuals, like me, marvel at these misunderstood creatures."

"You *know* I hate spiders," Jodi said, breaking into a cold sweat. "I even told you so. Why are you doing this to me?"

He dodged the question again. "Did I mention that Delilah's leg span is about twelve inches? That would be as large as a dinner plate, although by the looks of it you've lost your appetite." He laughed.

"You're not funny," Jodi stammered. She stole a glance in his direction. If fire could shoot out of her eyes, he'd be toast.

"I should also point out that these fine, orange hairs that cover her body are called setae," Dr. Blackstone said, carefully rotating the spider. "With them, Delilah can sting, like a bee. It's mainly a defensive reaction when confronted with hostility."

Jodi wanted to spit. "It's amazing she doesn't sting a snake like you."

"Come now, Jodi. This is very educational," Dr. Blackstone said with an evil grin. "Oh, there's one more thing. Delilah hunts by relying upon sensory organs located on her legs. When she feels the vibrations of her prey, she'll spray her dinner with a venom that serves a predigestive function. The venom isn't lethal, exactly. But the allergic reaction to it can be life-threatening."

Jodi's heart tried to leap out of her chest. She tossed back and forth trying to break free, but the more she wrestled with her bindings, the tighter they seemed to get. Her forehead began to drip with sweat.

"Now, let's review the rules of the game." Dr. Blackstone took a slow breath. "In a moment, I'll place Delilah on your stomach. Naturally, you don't want to make her skittish with any movement. Even a puff of air can agitate her. If you don't move, you don't get hurt. Any questions?"

Jodi had lots of them, but all she could manage was, "Why?"

"Because, Jodi, I'm trying to help you understand the position you're in. You're sticking your nose in where it doesn't belong."

He placed the spider on her stomach.

Although still fully dressed, Jodi froze. She didn't dare provoke the spider. *Oh God! Please help me!* she whispered.

"Right now," Dr. Blackstone said, "all you are is an interesting piece of new terrain. Move, and you become a threat, or, perhaps you'll resemble dinner. One can't predict such things. Of course, neither option is particularly good. So when in doubt, my advice is, don't move."

As Delilah made its way across Jodi's chest and up her neck, Dr. Blackstone maintained his icy narrative. "Of course, insects are at the top of their list. Crickets. Moths. Grasshoppers are a special treat.

Makes the meal more interesting when it runs, I suppose. Sometimes she'll eat pieces of beef heart, baby mice, or small snakes."

Jodi wanted to scream.

She wanted to run.

She wanted to cover her face with her hands. But the underside of the spider, and its armlike appendages, was already doing a good job of covering her face. Jodi kept telling herself, *Don't move . . . don't move . . . move and die!* It was then—her eyes directly under Delilah's hairy abdomen—that a new thought jumped into her mind. *The cell phone.* What if the caller tried again? Would the ring startle the spider? Would it overreact and, in panic, shoot Jodi with venom?

"How interesting," Dr. Blackstone said. "I see Delilah must be thirsty. Who would have thought she'd drink the sweat right off your forehead."

Jodi thought she was about to faint when Dr. Blackstone picked the spider up. She exhaled and then repeatedly gasped for air, gulping it as fast as her lungs could handle it.

"See, no harm done," Dr. Blackstone said, his tone impassive. "And why? Because you knew the rules of our game. Now look at me."

She looked.

"The game of life has rules, too, young lady." He paused. "Make a wrong move and you'll get hurt. In other words, it would be most prudent of you to refrain from your current course of action regarding what you saw at the rave."

He leaned his mouth close to her right ear and lowered his voice a notch. "Now, I'm about to release you, Miss Jodi Adams of 1414 Spring Creek Drive. I'm sure your parents, Jack and Rebecca, are nice people, too. Remember, further nosing around will provoke a lethal response. Have I been clear?"

A hot tear rolled down Jodi's face.

The moment Jodi walked out the front door of the Pet Vet Wellness Center, she wanted to run. And run. And run. She wanted to go home and pack her family and move to a deserted island halfway around the world. Whatever it took to put as much distance between the evil operation of Dr. Blackstone and her family, she'd do it in a heartbeat.

How did he know where I lived? Jodi wondered, eyeing the parking lot for her car. *He even knew my parents' names!* Of minor comfort was the thought that her parents, thankfully, were out of town at her grandmother's house for the day.

Jodi found herself suddenly standing beside her car. She didn't remember crossing the parking lot. She was functioning on autopilot. She reached into her front pants pocket for her keys, withdrew them, and then promptly dropped them on the ground. She picked them up and, hand outstretched, pushed the remote keyless entry button several times.

Nothing. Frustrated, she stomped her right foot.

Fearful that Dr. Blackstone might have changed his mind, she stole another look over her shoulder. There wasn't going to be a Round Two of Beauty and the Beast, not if she could help it. She looked back at the locked car. Her hands shook so bad, she had difficulty inserting the right key into the driver's lock.

Get a grip, girl! she said to herself out loud. On the third try, she unlocked the car and then slipped behind the wheel. Once inside, she locked the doors and struggled to put the key in the ignition at the same time. In truth, she was shaking more from what she knew than what she had endured with the spider.

The engine roared to life. But Jodi, her mind racing, remained parked. She managed to put the car in reverse and started to back up when she almost rammed into a large, dark black SUV with tinted windows that sped behind her. She pounced on the brakes and took another deep breath to quiet the pounding in her chest.

More than ever, she needed to get out of there and put her hands on those photos. Nothing else mattered. Somewhere lurking in her subconscious was the notion that her photos were the proof she needed to link Dr. Blackstone to Kat's seizure and the wrongful death of the boy.

Why else would the doctor try to scare her silly?

As she pulled into traffic on Philmont Avenue from the clinic's parking lot, Jodi dialed Bruce on her cell phone. It rang several times.

"Hello?"

"Bruce . . . It's Jodi. Boy am I glad I caught you. Where are you?"

"Pep Boys."

"Excuse me?"

"It's an auto parts store—"

"Uh, okay, look. We really need to . . . meet somewhere, like, now or sooner." Her voice trembled.

"What's wrong, Jodi? You sound pretty shook up? Is it Kat?"

"I am kind of a mess, and no. Kat's okay—or was this morning when I left." Was it really this morning when she had sat across from Kat in the hospital? Seemed like an eternity.

"You had lunch yet?"

"No." Jodi studied her rearview mirror.

"How about we meet in ten minutes at the Dairy Queen on Philmont."

"Perfect. That's right near, um, where I've got to pick up my film. See you then."

Jodi hung up and then tucked the phone under her left leg. She drove in silence for several blocks. *Bruce must think I'm a basket case,* she thought. *Maybe I am.*

Then again, who wouldn't be? She had a friend in the hospital on life support; she'd stumbled onto a dead boy who, in turn, disappeared without a trace; she'd met two policemen who were either incompetent or on the take; and, to top it off, she'd just costarred in her own private horror movie with a giant spider.

Maybe Bruce was right. Maybe she should just drop the whole thing. Kat was safe and that's what mattered, right? If some kid died at the event, why should that concern her? If Dr. Blackstone wanted to manufacture illegal drugs, why should she care? Live and let live. Look out for Number One, right? Wasn't that the message Mrs. Meyer preached at school?

Jodi pulled her car into the parking lot of the mini strip mall, a nondescript collection of stores where the InstyFoto Mart was located. *Perfect timing,* she thought as a small Ryder truck was just starting to pull out of a spot in front of the store.

She slowed to a stop, allowing the truck to pass. As it approached, she thought the driver looked vaguely familiar. She shielded her eyes from the brilliant sun. The truck passed her. *Boy, that guy sure looked like Reverend Bud,* she thought.

What was he doing at the photo mart? Then again, maybe it was her imagination. She pulled into the vacant spot, turned off the engine and, for the first time, felt as if she could breathe without the aid of a respirator. She exhaled a long, cleansing breath.

Jodi gathered up her purse, cell phone, and keys. Grabbing the door handle, she paused. Since Dr. Blackstone knew about her encounter with the police, then Officer Dexter and Sergeant Schmidt were probably linked to him. If so, then their relationship with Dr. Blackstone was a little too cozy for comfort. Was there money somehow involved?

What's more, Carlos had said he worked for Reverend Bud. So, if the cops—who, for the sake of argument, probably knew Dr. Blackstone—were looking the other way on the drug dealing at the rave, it would be reasonable to infer that Dr. Blackstone and Reverend Bud might be working together somehow. But how?

Her eyebrows remained tightly knit into a knot.

And how did the syringes fit in? According to Bruce, they were an exact match to those used by the clinic. Plus, didn't Bruce say they were filling batches of syringes with that keta-stuff for other clinics? Now she wasn't so sure. What if they were never intended to be sold to other animal hospitals and instead were sold to kids at the rave? She'd run her theory past Bruce.

Jodi stepped out of the car, locked the door, and then ducked into the InstyFoto Mart. At the counter, she looked through her purse but couldn't find her film stub.

"How can I help you?" the clerk asked.

Jodi didn't answer. Piece by piece, she emptied the contents on the glass counter. "It's got to be here," she said under her breath.

"Are you picking up or dropping off?"

Jodi looked up and then examined his nametag: Mike.

"Um, Mike, I seem to have misplaced my claim check," Jodi said, shaking her head in disbelief. The syringe was also missing. *That's really weird*, she thought. She knew she hadn't left either item at home. *Maybe they fell out in the car.* She continued to fumble through her things.

"That's not a problem," Mike said. "What's the last name?"

"Adams. Jodi Adams. I . . . I dropped off a disposable camera this morning."

Mike smiled. "Oh, well, you don't have anything to worry about."

"I don't?" Jodi stopped her search. Their eyes met.

"Actually, your brother already picked up the film," Mike said. His smile was pleasant. "In fact, you just missed him."

Jodi bristled. "I don't have a brother."

'm late, aren't I?" Jodi said, out of breath as she slipped into the seat across from Bruce. She ran her fingers through her hair.

"No prob. I just ordered a hamburger—"

Jodi interrupted. "You'll never believe what happened, like, a minute ago—"

"Time-out," Bruce said, making a T-sign with his hands. "You better order something. You look seriously pale."

"Do I really look that bad?" Jodi looked at her face in the stainless-steel napkin holder.

"Let's just say if you're anything like the typical female, I highly doubt you'd go to the mall in this, um, condition," Bruce said.

"Well, if you'd been through what I've just gone through—," Jodi said, touching her face.

The waitress served Bruce his burgers and fries and then turned to Jodi. "Can I get something for ya, hon?"

Jodi leaned her head to one side. "Okay. I'll splurge. I'd like one of your strawberry shakes . . . please. Thanks."

The server scribbled a note. "It'll be just a minute." She turned and left.

"So what's the big news?" Bruce gulped his soda.

Jodi looked around the restaurant and then leaned forward. "Okay, but first you've got to promise not to tell a soul."

"You know me," Bruce said, holding up three middle fingers. "Scout's honor."

"Let me tell you something, Bruce. This isn't a joke. These guys are serious—"

"Whoa. Slow down. What guys? Serious about what?"

"Okay . . . okay." Jodi placed both hands palms down on the table. "Remember how I took photos last night?"

"Mm-hmm." Bruce's mouth was full.

"I went to pick them up, like, five minutes ago and guess who I saw?" Jodi said.

"Britney Spears?"

"Knock it off, Bruce, I mean it." Jodi stared at him.

"All right already. I'll behave," Bruce said, smearing extra mustard on his burger. "You were saying . . ."

Jodi lowered her voice just above a whisper. "I saw Reverend Bud. He was there!"

Bruce shrugged. "Who?"

"Reverend Bud. The longhaired guy in charge of the rave." Jodi searched his eyes.

"Hey, like, I never met him, remember? I was at the hospital with Kat."

Jodi thought about that for half a second. "Well, anyway, he swiped *my* photos. I'd sure like to know why he'd do that. And how did he know about them?"

"Are we playing twenty questions?"

"Sometimes you can be so unbelievably moronic." Jodi looked away.

Bruce put his hamburger down and wiped his hands on his pants. "Listen, Jodi, I'm sorry. I . . . I just got carried away. So what else is bothering you?"

Jodi wasn't sure whether to tell Bruce about her experience with Dr. Blackstone. He'd probably just make a joke of it and she was in no mood to kid around. Couldn't he see what she was driving at?

"Come on, try me." Bruce reached across the table and tapped her on the hand.

"Well, the skinny is, um, I went to see Dr. Blackstone, just like you told me to do." Jodi tested the water before jumping in.

"Uh-huh."

"By the way," Jodi said, "you weren't there. What gives?"

Bruce raised his hands defensively. "Dr. Blackstone told me there must have been a scheduling mix-up and I wasn't scheduled to work. He told me to go home."

"Whatever," Jodi said. "He took me to his office and asked me a bunch of questions about what happened last night . . . about the syringe and the dead boy."

Bruce nodded. "He did the same thing with me." He popped a fry in his mouth.

"Yeah, but did he spike your drink and strap you to a table?"

Bruce leaned his head to one side. "You're telling me he—"

"And that's not all," Jodi said. "When I woke up, I was strapped to the table—like I said, and he, like, scared the life out of me with his giant orange spider . . . he let it crawl right over my face."

Bruce's face looked pained. "You've got to stop making stuff up, Jodi."

"So you don't believe me?" She sat on her hands. "I bet you don't know he has pet tarantulas . . ."

"Sure I do, but you have to admit," Bruce said, "it's kinda far out that he'd do all that to you. Maybe you suffer from arachnophobia or something." Bruce started to pour half a bottle of catsup over his fries, but stopped and put the bottle down.

A stiff moment passed between them.

"Look, Jodi. You've got to cut me some slack here. Before you sat down I thought this was all about stolen drugs. Then, out of the blue, you're saying that my boss is a psycho. Okay, so let's say I buy what you're saying," Bruce said. "Why would Dr. Blackstone do something so stupid, you know, that could get him sued?"

"Honestly? I still think it has something to do with those syringes you guys have been stocking . . ."

"Which are just like the ones we found at the rave—"

"Exactly," Jodi said. "Which means I think somehow your boss

and that Reverend Bud guy are, like, working together or something."

"And, if what you're thinking is true," he added, "then they
might both be implicated in the death of that kid . . . Hmm." Bruce
scratched his head.

"Bingo." Jodi thought they were finally getting somewhere.

"Here you go, honey," the waitress said, placing a tall strawberry
shake with whipped cream and a cherry on top in front of Jodi.
"You let me know if you need anything else," she said, withdrawing
a straw from the black apron around her waist.

"Thanks," Jodi said and then plucked the cherry off the top and
placed it on her napkin. "Those will kill you."

"I'll take my chances," he said with a laugh. He reached over and
picked up the cherry by the stem. "Wait a minute," he said. His
hand froze midair. "Do you still have your syringe?"

"Nope," Jodi said with a half frown. "I think your boss must have,
like, stolen it from my purse when I was drugged. Come to think
of it, I bet he took the claim check then, too. How about you? Still
have yours?"

"Syringe? No. I gave it to Dr. Blackstone for analysis . . . I mean,
how was I to know?" Bruce ate the cherry.

"You didn't." Jodi stuck the straw into her shake. "So we're left
with no evidence, right?"

"We?"

"Hey, you're not gonna just walk away—not now, are you?"

Bruce bit his bottom lip. "Um, remind me, why we can't, like, let
it go? I mean, this is all just a guess on our part . . . I've got, um, a
good job that pays decent cash. What if we're wrong?"

Jodi took a long slurp from her shake. "What if we're right?"

"Hey, I don't stand a chance here," Bruce said, raising his hands
as if surrendering. "You're only the debate champ for, what, the
whole state? So, like, I'm not trying to win an argument. Really. I'm
just curious why this is such an issue for you."

"I can sum it up in two words: *It stinks*."

"Sure does—"

"You can say that again," Jodi said. "What if that dead boy was your brother? I mean, he has a real name. He's got somebody somewhere wondering where he is—probably at this very moment, you know? They may never find out the truth unless we, like, piece things together."

"Unless *we*?" Bruce said, raising an eyebrow. "Since when did you and I become Batman and Robin?"

"Bruce, we're talking about a lack of justice here," Jodi said. "Anyway, I've done a little Bible study of my own . . . on justice. There's a verse in Psalms. You know what it says? 'Blessed are they who maintain justice, who constantly do what is right.'"

"So this is what you meant last night when you said it was a 'God thing.'" Bruce pushed his dish to the side.

"Yeah, sort of," Jodi said with a nod. "Sorry if I sounded preachy—"

"No, that's all good."

"Well, for me," Jodi said, bringing a hand to her chest, "I happen to believe in stuff like justice . . . and in right and wrong, because those things are real important to God, you know? Let's just say that's why I won't give up."

"But aren't you just a little scared?" Bruce asked.

Jodi ran her fingers through her hair. "Yeah, like, only out of my mind!"

everend Bud sat in the Ryder truck. The rear bumper rested against the loading dock of the Pet Vet Wellness Center. His eyes were closed and his head leaned back. His left arm rested on the door. The workers had finished unloading the back of the truck. How he wished he could unload what was on his mind.

An oriole perched in a nearby pine sang a soothing melody that drifted into the cab while the smoke from a freshly lit joint floated out. A bead of sweat formed a line across Reverend Bud's creased forehead. He knew today he'd have to face the music.

Dr. Blackstone appeared at his window. "This is no time for a nap."

Reverend Bud blew a steady stream of gray smoke out of his nose. "A good afternoon to you, too, Dr. B." His eyes remained closed.

"Listen to me," said Dr. Blackstone. "Better yet, look at me when I'm talking to you. I've got just a minute. Illya and Zhenya will be back in a couple of hours and I've got to prepare their shipment. Thanks to your work last night, it will be sizable."

Reverend Bud's head swiveled to the left. His eyes rolled halfway open. A drop of sweat fell from his brow and landed in the thicket of his beard.

Dr. Blackstone brought a cigar to his mouth. He withdrew a gold lighter from the pocket of his black khakis and, with a metallic *click*, flicked open the top. A flame danced in place. "I'm thinking it's time to plan another Mystery Rave—next month when the schools let out for the summer." He waved the lighter around as he spoke. "Kids will be bored and ready to party. We've done the beach and the mountains. This time how about the quarry? There's an abandoned quarry—"

"Not that. Definitely not that."

"The possibilities are endless," Dr. Blackstone said, lighting the premium cigar. He puffed several times. "Even for an idealist like you."

"Dude, I've been thinking . . ."

"That's always dangerous," Dr. Blackstone said with a laugh. He blew a thick cloud in the direction of Reverend Bud.

"For real. See, I keep telling myself this isn't the way things are supposed to be . . . I mean, I was minding my own business, doing raves, spreading the good vibes. Plenty of Peace, Love, Unity, and Respect to go around. Then we meet—"

"And look at you now," Dr. Blackstone said between puffs. "Your raves are huge successes."

"Sure, things got ramped up. More people and all. But, well, to be honest, I'm tired of playing taxi driver for the Grim Reaper, you dig?" He brushed his long hair away from his face.

"What are you saying?"

"Things are way too crazy now and I . . . I want out . . . I'm done with this money grab."

"You know what your problem is?" Dr. Blackstone shook his head, disgusted. He pointed with the end of his cigar at Reverend Bud. "You're afraid of money."

"You're way wrong, man." Reverend Bud took another drag from his joint. He held his breath for a moment before exhaling.

"Enlighten me." Dr. Blackstone raised an eyebrow.

"Dude, don't you fear God? Doesn't what we're doing bother you in the least?"

Dr. Blackstone savored a long draw from the cigar, leaving it in his mouth as he spoke. "What are you driving at?"

Reverend Bud shut his eyes, deep in thought. A picture of his father behind the pulpit surfaced through the fog in his mind.

"'What good will it be for a man if he gains the whole world, yet forfeits his soul?'"

"Excuse me?"

"That's from the Bible, Dr. B." His eyes shot open as if he had witnessed a ghost. "I've seen the light and we've sold our souls, man. For what? The Almighty Dollar? A nice house? Plenty of chicks? Well, I say, forget that, you know? Chuck it all," he said with a wave of his hand. "Keep my share from last night. I don't really care 'cause I'm, like, outta here."

Dr. Blackstone, his cigar pinched between his thumb and fore-finger, spit on the ground. "Save your platitudes for someone who cares. You're not going anywhere."

"Watch me."

Their eyes locked.

"If I were you," Dr. Blackstone said slowly, "I'd be very careful not to rock the boat, and especially not with the Russians."

Reverend Bud looked straight ahead and shouted with the flair of a prophet, "'The Lord says, "Do not be afraid of those who kill the body but cannot kill the soul. Rather, be afraid of the One who can destroy both soul and body in hell."'"

"Oh, shut up!" Dr. Blackstone glared. "Nobody knows what we're doing. Nobody needs to know. Now, if you're done with this religious mumbo jumbo—"

Reverend Bud ignored him. "The Good Book says, 'For God will bring every deed into judgment, including every hidden thing, whether it is good or evil.'"

"Stop it . . . stop it, I say!" Dr. Blackstone pounded his hand against the side of the truck.

Reverend Bud was on a roll. Somehow the release felt good. "'But I tell you that it will be more bearable for Sodom on the day of judgment than for you.'"

Dr. Blackstone bared his teeth like a dog with rabies. Smoke from his cigar curled up around his nose. "All I can say is, you're a fool."

Reverend Bud laughed. "'But God said to him, "You fool! This very night your life will be demanded from you."'"

Dr. Blackstone's face reddened. He grabbed Reverend Bud's arm and squeezed it like a vise. "I don't know what's come over you. Maybe you're tired. You're definitely high. But you'll be a dead man if you walk."

Reverend Bud swallowed. "Dude, like, why are you so afraid of a little soul-searching? Huh?"

Dr. Blackstone, flushed with anger, looked up at the sky and then toward the clinic. "You're making a giant mistake."

"I don't think so, man. Now if it's all the same to you"—Reverend Bud turned the key in the ignition—"I'm gonna skedaddle, dig?"

"Sure. Go right ahead. It's your funeral."

Dr. Blackstone rammed the cigar back between his teeth.

Jodi collapsed behind the wheel of her car, discouraged. Bruce had given her such a hard time over lunch. If he, of all people, had his doubts, who else would believe her? To make matters worse, her film was stolen and the needle had been swiped.

She was confident Dr. Blackstone had something to do with the missing syringe, but there was no point in making an accusation. It would come down to her word against his. Besides, the only way she'd ever set foot in that clinic again would be if three men armed with stun guns and a straitjacket dragged her there.

She took a deep breath and then started the car. "Jesus," she said softly, her hand on the gearshift, "if you don't want me to drop this, I'm going to need a minor breakthrough here. Please give me at least *something* to go on. Amen."

She looked over her shoulder and then backed up the car. She shifted into DRIVE and pulled out of the parking lot onto Philmont Avenue. Jodi was headed back to Abington Hospital. At least she could see if Kat's condition had stabilized. And maybe, if Kat was more alert, Jodi could find out what the boy's name was, or at least where he went to school. If Kat knew at least that much, Jodi thought, she could find his picture in an old yearbook and confirm his identity. *And then what?* Jodi wondered.

Traffic was light, especially for a holiday weekend. She'd make the hospital in ten or fifteen minutes. She switched on the radio to pass the time, and the car instantly filled with sound. She could tell without looking at the digital readout that the dial was set to 1060

AM, home of KYW News Radio. It was her dad's favorite station.

Jodi's finger was about to hit the scan button when something the announcer said caught her ear midsentence:

. . . has learned the popular club drug ecstasy, a so-called feel-good drug, mixed with ketamine, an animal tranquilizer, may have played a part in the disappearance of Todd Rice, a seventeen-year-old, Abington High School junior. Sources say Todd Rice attended an illegally sponsored rave in an abandoned warehouse on Christopher Columbus Boulevard last night.

Jodi's fingers raced to turn up the volume. Her eyes were on the road, but scenes from the rave filled her mind.

Todd's parents, Keith and Allison Rice, were first alerted to his disappearance by several friends who had carpooled with him to the rave. His friend Holly, who didn't want her last name used, told KYW: "Everybody was all, like, partying. I was doing some E and stuff when Todd said he wanted to try a little Special K, just for fun. That's the last time I saw him."

Jodi slowed the car and pulled over to the side of the road. She didn't want to miss a single word. The announcer continued with his report.

Susie Shenkel, another friend of the missing teenager, told KYW: "Yeah, we were all freaking out. We were standing around for an hour trying to find him. I mean, Todd was our ride and we were supposed to leave at seven. When we couldn't find him, we didn't know what to do. So we, like, called his home and he wasn't there, either."

Todd's mother, Allison, called authorities at ten o'clock when he failed to come home: "Todd's always been a good kid . . . He's never . . . done drugs . . . at least none that we knew about. We thought, well, we *assumed* Todd went dancing, you know, at a local club. We were so shocked when . . . when his friends called this morning. We had no idea he'd been involved in . . . anyway, now he's missing and we're so worried . . ."

The tears in Allison's voice poured out of the radio. Jodi felt a tightness in her chest, knowing that if Todd was the same kid she and Bruce saw last night, then he wasn't just missing, he was dead. Jodi rested her head against the window as she listened, although she probably knew more than the reporter—like her contact with Reverend Bud, Dr. Blackstone, the brain-dead police—and that, coupled with this news, was far more than she could digest at the moment.

Special K is the street name for ketamine. When mixed with ecstasy, users call that cocktailing. In humans, while ketamine can have a hallucinogenic effect, it can also lead to death. Both substances are illegal for sale or use by the public.

No wonder Dr. Blackstone wanted us stopped, Jodi thought. A memory of the spider's hairy legs crawling all over her face crept into her mind. She swatted at the mental picture.

His parents say Todd left the house last night wearing jeans, sneakers, and a white T-shirt with the Disney character Tweety Bird. Any person with information should call our KYW Tipline. This has been a Special KYW News Bulletin. Updates as they happen, when they happen. For a look at traffic . . .

Jodi switched off the radio. Her heart was in hyperspace; thoughts whirled inside her head. Since going to the police was out of the question, now what? Should she call KYW? Should she contact Todd's parents? They were probably listed in the phone book. But what would she tell them?

Somehow none of the options felt right. How would anyone believe her without concrete proof? She needed those photos, and there was only one way to get them back.

Jodi reached across the front seat for her purse, her fingers moist with sweat. She picked up the purse and then flipped open the clasp. Like a detective rummaging around for a key piece of evidence, she dug through the contents.

A moment later Jodi said, "Yes!" She held up the business card Reverend Bud had handed her last night. Sure enough, just as she remembered, it listed his address and phone number. She reread the inscription: Peace, Love, Unity, Respect, and that bizarre offer for a free tablet of ecstasy.

If what was printed was to be believed, he lived or had an office on Rawle Street in northeast Philly. She knew the general area. A collection of modest but older row homes about twenty minutes away. She decided to try what always worked in her debate situations: confront the opponent head-on.

She snatched up her phone as her pulse quickened. Just as she was about to dial his number, her cell phone rang. She jumped at the sound, sending her purse, which had been balanced on her lap, to the floor. The contents spilled in every direction. She composed herself and took a close look at the number provided by her caller I.D., but didn't recognize it. Probably a telemarketer.

"Hello?"

Silence. She waited a second. "Hello?"

"Um, is this Jodi?"

"Yes." She pressed the phone against her ear. The voice sounded hollow and distant.

"Cool. Um, we need to meet."

"I'm sorry, do I know you?" Her tone was tentative.

"Oh, right. It's Reverend Bud. We met last night—"

Her skin jumped like a cat on a hot tin roof. "How did you get this number?"

"Chill, babe. Like . . . oh . . . yeah, remember your photo order? The envelope had your info on the wrapper."

The sudden feeling of being violated darted through her veins. *So it* was *Reverend Bud at the InstyFoto Mart,* she thought. "What gave you the right to steal my pictures?"

"See, I . . . I did you a favor—"

"Really? How so? This ought to be good."

"I don't have much time left, and, um, wow, we need to hook up. Like now. You dig?"

"You didn't answer my question. How was swiping my stuff doing me a favor?" Jodi fixed her eyes on a tube of lipstick that had rolled beneath the brake pedal.

"Okay, okay. I'll"—he coughed—"tell you all that jive when we connect. You still got, um, my card?"

His business card in her hand suddenly felt like a time bomb. "Yes. I . . . gee, I don't know about meeting." It was one thing for her to take the lead, but this felt like an ambush.

"Look," Reverend Bud said, "what I'm trying to say . . . see, the same people who are . . ." He stopped midsentence.

Jodi examined the phone to make sure they weren't cut off. She brought it back to her ear. "You still there? The same people who are what?"

". . . watching you are after me. See, I know about the body and, um, way more than that, you dig?"

That caught her off guard. *I'm being watched?* she thought. "How can I know you're telling the truth? I mean, we've only met once." Jodi switched the phone to her left ear. He sounded sincere enough, but one never knew about these things.

"I don't know . . . you'll just have to trust me, babe. But hurry, there isn't much time before I'm . . . gone." The connection went dead.

Jodi's heart hammered away. Was he weaving his own web of lies, trying to draw her in? For what? To scare her like Dr. Blackstone? Yet she was fairly certain she had detected some emotion in his voice. What was it? Fear? Sadness? A heavy heart? Although she couldn't put her finger on it, she sensed Reverend Bud wanted to come clean. She had to go. What other option did she have?

Jodi had to remember to breathe. She rested the phone on the dash and then picked up the spilled contents of her purse from the floor. She checked her rearview mirror and then dialed a number before pulling back into traffic.

"Yo."

"Hey, Bruce, you busy? It's Jodi."

"Not really. I'm at a pet store. Thought I'd start collecting a few spiders . . ."

"Very funny. Listen. KYW just did a story on the missing boy."

"The stiff?"

"Come on, Bruce, this is important."

"Since when did you become a news junkie?"

"I'm not—and never mind that." Jodi shook her head. "I've got the boy's name. It's Todd Rice. He didn't come home last night."

"How can you be sure he's, like, the same guy?"

"His mom gave a description of what Todd was wearing. Remember the Tweety Bird shirt?"

"Sure, but why are you telling me this?"

"Hold on. There's one more thing. You'll never believe who just called me."

"Elvis?"

"No, you dork. Reverend Bud. He's that longhaired guy—"

"I remember. So what's his deal?"

Jodi paused to frame her thoughts. "Um, he admitted he took my photos and he wants to meet me. He said he knows all about the body and a whole bunch more. I . . . well, I thought I'd see if you'd go with me. Will you?"

Bruce didn't hesitate. "Sounds about as attractive as earwax."

"You sure?" Jodi stopped at a red light.

"Without a doubt . . . 100 percent positively no way. See, in the grand scheme of things, I'm not the one on the mission from God, here."

Jodi stared out the windshield at the cars passing by, uncertain of what to say. The light changed to green.

"I mean," Bruce added, "I think it's great that you—"

"Never mind, Bruce." Jodi closed her eyes as she focused on the fact she was going to face Reverend Bud alone. "Listen, I've got to go. We'll talk later." She hung up.

At least Jodi *hoped* there would be a later.

n the twenty-three minutes it took Jodi to make her way across town, her heart had skipped a beat at least once a minute. Now, within several blocks of Reverend Bud's house, it tapped away with the intensity of a Mexican hat dance.

Jodi made the turn off East Roosevelt Boulevard onto Longshore Avenue. She glanced in her rearview mirror. Was she really being watched? Reverend Bud had said as much. But could he be trusted to tell the truth? She had checked her mirrors a dozen times since leaving Huntingdon Valley. It didn't seem anybody was tailing her. Then again, if she had been shadowed, he'd be a pro. She was just a kid in the minor leagues—and she knew it.

Jodi slowed her car to double-check the address on Reverend Bud's business card: 73 Rawle Street.

She turned right on Sackett and studied the numbers. She was headed in the right direction when suddenly Jodi realized she would much rather have her tonsils removed—or bungee jump off the Betsy Ross Bridge—than face Reverend Bud alone. She didn't have so much as a Bic lighter for the purposes of self-defense. Where was Phil Meyer when she needed him?

It wasn't that she felt Reverend Bud would actually attack her. He might, like Dr. Blackstone, just try to scare her off. If Dr. Blackstone was into spiders, then perhaps Reverend Bud was into snakes. One thing was certain, she wouldn't drink anything offered to her this time.

She made a left onto Rawle.

As she passed the row homes that lined both sides of the street, she took some comfort knowing there were plenty of neighbors who might come to her rescue—if they could hear her through the thick plaster and lath walls.

Jodi's history teacher, who lived around the corner, had once told her that these row homes had been built in the late 1930s during a time when neighbors actually enjoyed each other's company; when closeness and community were preferred over sprawling lawns and tall fences.

Jodi remembered attending an old-fashioned block party with her teacher and her history classmates. While the disc jockey spun the tunes, the neighbors, mostly Irish Catholics and Italians, consumed plates piled high with kielbasa, bratwurst, sausage, and peppers, and homemade potato salad. Kids danced in the street, at least those who weren't throwing water balloons. Togetherness was part of the fabric of community life.

But today, while she was an invited guest, this was no party.

She checked the house and street number again: 77 Rawle.

The closer she got to her destination, the more she felt as if she were entering a restricted biohazard site where the potential for personal harm ranked up there with the odds of paying taxes. Yet each time she entertained the thought of heading in the opposite direction as fast as possible, she was encouraged by something she had read in the Psalms that morning. She whispered the words aloud, "I will go in the strength of the Lord."

For Jodi, to repeat the words of the psalmist wasn't like rubbing a good luck charm, or an exercise in positive thinking, or repeating a mantra to invoke a magic spell. Jodi viewed her "mission from God," as Bruce had said, as exactly that. Since God had placed on her heart a burden for justice, she'd fulfill the mission in his strength.

Jodi slowed the Mazda to a crawl. She spotted the correct address and parked across the street behind a yellow Ryder truck. A tall, street-level tree partially obscured her view of Reverend Bud's row home. From what she could see, it appeared to be a clone of all the others on the block.

His was a flat-roofed, two-story brick home sandwiched between similar-looking units. Red and green curved Italian lap tiles covered the eaves. The grass in his front yard, which, she guessed, would barely have enough room to hold a picnic table and grill, was uncut. She eyed a rusted air-conditioning unit that dangled from a window on the second floor. The window blinds were closed.

She took a deep breath, placed her purse under the front seat, grabbed her phone and keys, and got out of the car. She locked the doors and crossed the street. As she approached Reverend Bud's house, a dog began to bark in the house next door. *This is really stupid. What am I doing here?*

At the top of the four concrete steps leading to the front door, she stood and reached over to ring the doorbell. She quickly discovered it was missing. The hole it had once occupied was as empty as the feeling in her stomach. She knocked on the door instead. The door drifted inward as she tapped on its faded white surface.

"Hello? Anybody home?" As she stood on the threshold, a stale, thick odor, resembling burnt oregano mixed with fried plastic, was the only greeting she received. She clutched her phone against her chest.

When Reverend Bud didn't answer, she gently pushed open the door and stepped inside. The bare floorboards, which covered a landing about three feet square, creaked in protest. Her eyes took a few seconds to adjust to the darkness inside. *This is crazy*, she thought as her heart, like a Geiger counter, pegged the meter. All she wanted were those photos. She'd grab them and get going.

"Hello? Reverend Bud? It's Jodi."

Still no answer. Her eyes narrowed as she scanned the room for any signs of life. A tired-looking sofa sat under the front windows. The curtains were drawn shut behind it. The coffee table was littered with old pizza boxes and beer cans.

She noticed that the television set, perched on a board suspended between two upside-down milk crates, was off. To the right of the TV was a garbage can overflowing with discarded beer cans. It looked as if someone had been playing basketball with the empties but missed the trash half the time.

Jodi took several more steps into the den. She called, "Hello? Hello?" as she moved to the center of the room. The pale blue, threadbare carpet did little to cushion her steps. The room wasn't really threatening, she decided; it just needed a woman's touch. That didn't prevent her heart from leaping each time her foot stepped on a noisy section of flooring.

On the other side of the den, thanks to what little light snuck around the edges of the curtains, she noticed a sparsely furnished dining room with a staircase leading up to the second floor. She walked over to and then stood at the bottom of the stairs. Looking up, she called out, "Reverend Bud . . . hello . . . it's Jodi." Her hand rested on the railing as she decided whether or not to climb the steps. Without air conditioning, the house was warm and she began to perspire.

From this vantage point, she could see through a doorway into the kitchen. Her eyes zeroed in on a crack of light beneath a door at the far end. Since it was the only light on in the whole place, she figured it was worth exploring.

Jodi left the steps and walked into the kitchen, across the badly stained linoleum floor to the door. She reached for the handle, her heart on full alert, ready to jump out of her chest, and then opened the door. A narrow wooden staircase led to the basement below. The odor she'd first smelled was definitely more intense here at the top of the steps.

"Reverend Bud? You home?"

Jodi took a tentative step down. And then another. And another. She reached the bottom of the stairs and stood on the black-and-red-tiled floor. The air was cooler than upstairs, but it had a damp, musty edge to it. She saw a giant cockroach scamper across the floor. She clutched the railing and called again. "Listen, I . . . I came just as you asked."

Still no response. Maybe she had missed him. Maybe he'd ducked out for a pizza. Maybe he was sleeping. Or maybe this was his idea of a game. Whatever the reason, her nervous system was about to short-circuit. She was grateful that the naked light bulb, suspended from the low ceiling by an extension cord, was on.

She quickly scanned her surroundings. If Reverend Bud's place was anything like her history teacher's row home, to her left would be the door to the garage and beyond that the alley. To her right would be a space for a small storage area or home office. Straight ahead she could see the washer and dryer.

She walked to the right and stood in the doorway. She leaned her head into the room and saw Reverend Bud. She stifled a gasp, covering her mouth with her hand.

Reverend Bud was lying on a sofa. One arm rested across his chest, the other dangled over the edge of the sofa. His fingers held something loosely by the floor. An ashtray filled with cigarette butts rested near his hand. Smoke spiraled upward from the end of a smoldering butt.

She cleared her throat. "Hello?" Jodi tapped lightly on the doorframe. She couldn't tell if he was sleeping, or, more likely, from what she knew of him, tripping. His long brown hair covered his face like a sheepdog. His chest rose and fell with each breath. He was still wearing the Got E? T-shirt from last night. "Um, Reverend Bud, I . . ."

This wasn't part of the plan. She thought she was going to be handed the pictures, hear what he had to say, then leave. When he didn't respond, Jodi decided to scope out the room for herself. She hoped to find the photos and then get out as fast as possible.

The cramped space resembled an office. A nondescript-looking lamp stood in the corner, casting its meager light about the room.

The walls, covered with a cheap brown paneling, appeared buckled in places. A calendar was pinned directly to the paneling. His desk, a smallish, almost kid-size piece, was covered with papers stacked in no apparent order.

Jodi moved toward the desk, an eye still focused in his direction. She bit the inside of her lip as she reached out and gently lifted a few papers. To free up both hands, she tucked her cell phone into the front pocket of her blue jeans. As she worked, she started to feel lightheaded from the stench in the room. She looked around for a window to open for some fresh air, but there were none.

After what felt like an eternity, Jodi spotted the edge of the familiar yellow-and-red InstyFoto envelope. Could they be her pictures? She reached for the packet, opened it, careful not to draw attention to her activity, and then thumbed through the contents.

Excitement, like a flood, rushed through her veins. They were indeed her pictures—including several of Todd Rice. This was exactly what she needed. What more could she want? She tucked the envelope in her rear pocket and then turned to leave.

Behind her, Jodi heard a groan. Her heart jumped into her throat. She jerked her head around and saw Reverend Bud, still in the prone position, running his fingers through his hair. His head rolled slowly in her direction. His matted beard was damp with the saliva that dripped from the edge of his mouth. Their eyes met, although his eyes appeared to be unfocused and red around the edges.

"Jodi? Don't leave," Reverend Bud said, his voice groggy. He attempted to sit up, but settled for leaning on one arm. "Not yet . . . not before you know everything . . ."

Jodi couldn't think of one good reason to hang around, but plenty of reasons to get out of that basement cave *pronto*. She had the pictures, and if she had an ounce of good sense, she'd hoof it up the steps before something *did* happen. Jodi twirled a few strands of hair around her fingers.

"I really don't know what to say." Jodi took another step toward the door.

"I can see you're outta here," Reverend Bud said, now sitting fully upright on the sofa, although hunched over. "I dig it. But listen." He coughed, followed by a heavy dry heave. "See, it won't be long before I . . . um, assume room temperature." He held up the item in his hand for her to see.

Jodi placed a hand on the doorjamb to help steady her emotions. He was holding a hypodermic needle. She had an idea of what he might mean, but she didn't want to believe it.

"I . . . I'm not sure I follow," Jodi said.

He sighed and then started to rock in place. "I just took . . . my last trip this side of glory—"

"An overdose? You took an overdose on *purpose?*"

Reverend Bud waved her off. "Yeah, I'm glorybound," he said. "Got the whole LSD-heroin-ecstasy combo pack starting to flow through my veins. But let's not waste time with that, man. Do you know if . . . if you were followed?"

Jodi hesitated, partly out of concern over the fact that a man might actually be dying in front of her, and partly out of a fresh concern for her own safety.

"By whom?"

"Dr. B. . . . I heard him . . . he asked the Russians to keep an eye on you."

Jodi blinked wide eyes. "Dr. B.? You mean Dr. Blackstone?"

He nodded. "Julius—his bad, beastly self."

"What Russians?"

He answered softly. "You don't know . . . about all that, then, do you?" He brushed the hair away from his face with a slow, unsteady movement of his hand.

She wasn't sure how much to say she knew or didn't know. She folded her arms. "Maybe. What if I do?"

He laughed. A tired, sad laugh. "Oh, like if you did, you'd only find a cave in the jungle to hide out. They're animals, man, that's all." He reached down to the ashtray on the floor to retrieve the smoldering cigarette stub. He brought it to his dry lips for a drag, like a condemned man savoring his final cigarette.

Although Jodi stood just ten feet away, she was having a difficult time hearing Reverend Bud. His words slurred and ran into each other like a multicar accident. She crossed the room and stood near him at the end of the sofa, now that he seemed about as threatening as a houseplant.

"Listen, Reverend," Jodi said. She felt like a kid in the zoo standing next to the lions' cage. She forced herself to remain calm. "I'm really, like, confused here. Do you work for Dr. Blackstone?"

"We're partners, sort of. Man, things were so . . . groovy for a while. I thought I was hooked up with the cosmological program, you dig?"

"Um, no." Jodi was about to sit down, but one look at the condition of the sofa changed her mind.

"See, I was doing the raves . . . I picked the locations . . . booked the bands . . . did all that jive on my own." Reverend Bud's hand trembled as he held the cigarette. "The peeps came to expand their minds . . . um, through the healing powers of music and ecstasy . . . I got to spread PLUR my way, you dig?"

Jodi nodded. She didn't want to interrupt his flow, especially since she wasn't sure how long he'd remain coherent.

"'Cause I'm the Evangelist of Ecstasy," Reverend Bud said. "Then Dr. B. came along and things got crazy," he continued, stroking his beard. "The guy's a freakin' genius. Bam-o! Just like that . . . the crowds got huge. See, he had the cash and . . . um, ideas to help me promote."

"So, what's in it for him?" Jodi said, her eyebrow in a knot. "I mean, he owns a vet clinic."

Reverend Bud heaved out a cough and laughed at the same time. "Plenty, man. Dig this. The guy's like a mad scientist . . . got more brews and magical potions than a witch doctor on acid." Reverend Bud flashed a toothy grin.

Jodi had had a firsthand experience with one of Dr. Blackstone's brews but decided not to bring it up.

"And that clinic," Reverend Bud said, "it's just a cover. He mixes up Special K . . . and we sell it to the peeps and split the bread. I figure anything to help them party . . . to expand their minds to higher levels of consciousness . . . to be one with the greater cosmos . . . Man, I really believed we had a good thing going."

"So last night, did the police know all this?" Jodi folded her arms. She pushed the embarrassing memory out of her mind.

"Some things . . . like, the drug part. Man, we've been paying them to chill out for a year. You know, to look the other way—"

"So why'd you steal my pictures?"

He closed his eyes. His face scrunched in pain. "Had to get them before Dr. B. . . . he was gonna destroy them . . . he hated loose ends . . . sent his, um, his secretary to get 'em."

"I don't get it." Jodi shook her head, confused. The fumes from his cigarette weren't helping, either. "The cops were on your payroll, so, like, how would pictures of the needle matter?"

"Listen, babe." He looked up at her, his eyelids drooping halfway across his eyes. "Everything was cool until you zapped a picture of that *kid*. See, there was no way to trace anything to the upstanding, honorable Dr. B. Then you came along. Instant bad karma for the doctor. Plus"—he took a deep breath as he scratched the side of his head—"um, get my cell phone."

Jodi tossed him a puzzled look.

"Babe, in my top desk drawer . . . go snag my phone, dig?"

Jodi stepped lightly across the room, hooked her hair around her ears, and then opened the center desk drawer. She held it up. "Got it." She drifted back to his side, closer this time.

"No, you keep it . . . on the side, check out the little black button . . . it's got the, um, tape-looking thingy on it."

"Right here," Jodi said, examining the phone. "I see it. What about it?"

"Cool . . . oh, it's just a groovy feature . . . lets you record, like, five minutes of whatcha call it? Personal memos or whatever?"

"Really?" Jodi had never heard of that option before.

"Let's just say I happened to record my speaks with Dr. B. the other day." Reverend Bud held his cigarette in front of his mouth as he talked. He chuckled. "Boy, Dr. B. will pee his pants with what's on there . . . like the Good Book says, 'By your words you will be acquitted, and by your words you will be condemned.'"

"That's from Matthew," Jodi said.

"Give the lady a prize . . ."

"Gee, what am I missing here?" Jodi ran her fingers through her hair. "Why would you help me and then—" She paused, not knowing how to put it.

"Kill myself?" Reverend Bud finished her sentence. His face appeared drawn and ghostly pale.

"Well, yeah." Jodi's heart was on maximum spin. What could be so awful that a man would take his own life to avoid?

"Jodi—do you believe in God?" His eyes were suddenly enlarged.

"Huh?" Jodi guessed he must be tripping out. "Well, sure, actually I do. I believe in Jesus, too."

"I . . . I just pray Jesus can forgive me . . . for what I've done." Reverend Bud blew a cloud of smoke out through his nose and then dropped the butt in the ashtray. He leaned against the sofa back, hands resting in his lap.

"See, I can't keep going with Dr. B.'s trip," Reverend Bud said in quiet, confessional tones. "It's a nasty scene . . . Blackstone's a monster and, um, I can't walk away with what I know . . . not with the Russian barbarians—"

"What about them?" Jodi asked, afraid Reverend Bud would pass out.

"The bodies . . . what we did with . . . the bodies. It's flipped out, man . . . that kid in the picture? . . . I'm so sorry . . . he's next . . . just dropped him at Dr. B.'s, dig—" Reverend Bud's head rolled forward. His chin settled on his chest.

Jodi gasped. She could barely contain what she'd just heard. She couldn't tell if Reverend Bud was hallucinating and making the whole wild story up or—worse—he was telling the truth. If what he said was true, she was in way over her head.

She didn't want to leave him this way, but she knew she couldn't stay.

Still holding his cell phone and, with the photos tucked safely in her back pocket, she dashed out of the room, stumbled twice as she sprinted up the stairs, and then had to slow her pace in the darkness of the main floor. She bumped into the dining room table, fumbled her way through the den like a blind man, and managed to find the front door.

As Jodi burst out the door from darkness to light, fresh, pure air greeted her thankful lungs. Like a husky in deep snow, Jodi bounded across the street to her car. She was shuffling through her keys, when a ray of sunlight, reflecting off the windshield of a black Suburban, caught her eye. She jerked her head around and noticed the SUV had turned onto Rawle Street.

It was headed in her direction.

Something about it seemed vaguely familiar. Maybe the heavily tinted windows. Maybe the oversize tires. She couldn't quite pinpoint when she'd seen it last. She looked back at the jumble of keys she held with hands that were sticky with sweat. She trembled as she tried to identify the correct one.

As sudden as a bolt of lightning, the memory flashed back into her mind. She had seen the imposing vehicle as she had tried to back out of Dr. Blackstone's clinic earlier that morning.

A coincidence?

Her racing heart voted against that likelihood.

Jodi hopped in her car and pounced on the door lock.

Jodi closed her eyes for a moment, her mind on maximum spin. Reverend Bud had said she was being watched, but it was only now, with the armadillo-looking Suburban moving toward her, that the implication of her situation dawned on her. What if they were the Russians?

A sudden wave of panic washed over her. These were shark-infested waters. Her only chance at survival was to get out of harm's way, but how?

A new thought surfaced. It was entirely possible whoever was driving that beast came to inflict serious pain *not* on her, but on Reverend Bud. After all, she reasoned, nobody knew she was coming to visit Reverend Bud, except for Reverend Bud—and Bruce. She was fairly sure neither would have told a soul. What sense would it make for Reverend Bud to help her and then turn her over to the Russians?

Then again, maybe she was overreacting. What if they happened to live here? Could be a couple of kids out joyriding. There could be a thousand perfectly normal explanations for the presence of the Suburban. But Jodi didn't care to wait around to find out. As far as she was concerned, they *were* the Russians.

Jodi fired up the engine, snapped on her seat belt, and then checked her mirror. She saw the Suburban crawling slowly down the street. She guessed the driver was checking the street numbers.

Jodi gripped the wheel, paralyzed by fear for her safety and, at the same time, her concern for Reverend Bud. How could she just leave him like that? Was he dead? What if he was still alive, but just unconscious? If the Russians had come for him, he wouldn't have a chance, not in that condition.

She kicked herself for not checking his pulse.

A voice inside her head said, "What are you waiting for? *Go! GO! GO!!*"

Jodi put the car in gear and pulled away from the curb. Five seconds later, Jodi checked her mirror and noticed that the Suburban, now a half block behind her, had stopped in the middle of the street adjacent to Reverend Bud's house. She watched as both the driver and the passenger doors opened. Two men in black suits climbed out.

Jodi fished her cell phone out of her front pocket, swerving slightly as she did. Her hands shook as she tried to steer and dial 911 simultaneously. She hit the SEND button.

It rang forever, or so it seemed.

Jodi said out loud, "Come on, come on, come on. Today already!"

A dispassionate voice finally filled the earpiece.

"911 Operator. What is the nature of your emergency?"

"Um, there's a guy at 73 Rawle Street." Jodi's voice cracked as she spoke. "He's taken, like, a drug overdose."

"How long ago did this happen?"

Jodi was wearing her watch, but she had no sense of time. "I really can't say for sure. Like, maybe, half an hour ago?"

"Is the individual conscious?"

"No, ma'am." Jodi stopped at a stop sign. She used the moment to steal a look in the mirror. The two men pointed at the house and then in her direction before climbing back into their vehicle.

"Is he breathing?" The 911 operator's voice jarred her back into the conversation.

"I . . . I don't know for sure." Jodi's eyes danced between the road in front of her and the action in her rearview mirror.

"All right. Help is on the way. Where is he in the house?"

"Oh, he's in the basement in, like, an office . . . and you better hurry, 'cause I think there's some people coming to hurt him." Although, at the moment, it appeared the Russians were changing plans.

"Are you still with him?" The voice had no emotion.

"I'm . . . no, I'm not. I'm in my car. He's alone, or was when I left him a minute ago." This time, when Jodi looked back, the doors of the Suburban were closed. The monster truck was moving toward her, slow yet as ominous as a fiery lava flow.

"What is your name?"

Jodi hesitated. *My name? How about his?*

The operator spoke again. "I repeat, what is your name? Are you a relative?"

"Listen, I really can't talk right now. Just send help, and fast! Please?" Jodi hung up, shaking. She turned left and noticed the Suburban did the same thing about half a block behind her. Obviously, these guys had shifted their attention from Reverend Bud to her. But why? Did they know about the pictures in her pocket? Probably not. So why the sudden interest? And why did they just hang back instead of zooming up on her?

She placed her cell phone on her lap and grabbed the wheel with both hands. She had to think. She had to clear away the traffic jam of ideas inside her head. Most of all, she needed to get a grip. She was definitely no match for these characters, and she wasn't about to outrun them in her pint-size car.

Half in a panic, the only person she knew who might be capable of handling them was Phil Meyer. She'd call him. As an ex–Navy Seal, he'd know what to do—that is, *if* he was home.

Without warning, a large yellow, red, and green beachball rolled into the street several yards in front of her. Jodi hit the brakes and skidded to a stop. As she did, her cell phone, a thin, flip-up model, fell off her lap and crashed to the floor near the brake pedal. "Oh . . . *great!*"

Jodi watched the ball roll completely across the street. She started to drive again, propelled by the sight of the Russians on her tail, when several kids, without looking, darted into her path in a mad scramble for the ball.

"*Watch out!!*" Jodi screamed as she slammed the brakes again, this time more forcefully to avoid the children. As her foot hammered the pedal, she heard a cracking sound.

Her heart jumped.

She was afraid to look over the hood of her car.

Dear Jesus, did I hit them? she wondered. For a long minute, time vaporized as Jodi's emotions were stretched between the drama unfolding in front of her and, at the same time, behind her. To her surprise, there were no screams. There was no crying. And a minute later, the kids ran back to the sidewalk, ball in hand. Their giggles filled the air.

Thankful nobody was hurt, Jodi exhaled and then reached down for her phone. When she picked it up, she discovered her heel had mashed it. Her heart sank.

"Now what?" she said out loud with one eye trained on the black Suburban closing in behind her. How was she going to call Phil? How was she going to call *anybody?*

"What a dork!"

✳ ✳ ✳

"Zhenya, too near," Illya said, chewing on a sunflower seed in the front passenger seat of the Suburban. "Give girl space."

Illya consulted an object in his hand. It was a Global Positioning System display the size of a Palm Pilot. He was puzzled. The GPS tracked several devices, including Reverend Bud's cell phone. They had gone to teach Reverend Bud a lesson in loyalty and, until now, the GPS indicated he was at home. But, shortly after they arrived, the signal moved away from his address.

Illya held a set of high-powered binoculars to his eyes. He could see the label sticking up from the back of Jodi's shirt, although he didn't know who she was.

Illya lowered the binoculars. "I say you what I think," Illya said, spitting out the shell.

Zhenya grunted.

"I say Comrade Bud lay down in backseat, *da?*"

"*Da.*"

Illya consulted the GPS again and then shook his head, changing his mind. "Perhaps no. Perhaps trunk?"

"*Da.*" Zhenya reached inside his coat pocket for a cigarette. "Smoke?"

"*Nyet.*" Illya waved him off and then raised the field glasses to his face.

Zhenya lit up.

"So, blondie, you going where now?" Illya said to himself.

✳ ✳ ✳

More than anything, Jodi wanted to tap her heels together three times and wake up behind the controls of an armored tank. Or, better yet, in her bed, discovering this was all just a bad dream. She settled for the option of stepping on the gas pedal.

The engine whined. It strained and started to sputter like a lawn mower in wet grass, followed by a chiming sound.

What's up with that? she wondered. Jodi scanned the dash and froze at the sight of the now illuminated, miniature orange gas pump in the lower right-hand corner of the instrument panel.

The idiot light signaled she was almost out of gas.

"You've probably got a little more than one gallon left," her dad had said the last time this happened. "At least that's my best esti-mate," she recalled him saying.

Jodi pounded the steering wheel with both hands in unison. "So that's the way it's gotta be? Huh, God?" Jodi couldn't stop the sud-den flow of tears from rolling down her cheeks.

"I mean . . . for all I know, my friend Kat's dying in a hospital at this very second. And, Reverend Bud's, like, dying back there somewhere. That kid, um, Todd, he's already dead. And, gee whiz . . . I'm only running for my life—with a car that's outta gas. I really, like, need a break here."

Jodi wiped away the tears with the back of her hand.

"I don't know, God. Maybe I should pull over, promise to keep my big mouth shut, and just give those Russians my photos . . . is that what you want?" Jodi sniffled and then dabbed at her eyes with a leftover napkin she had plucked out of the glove compartment.

All this time she had been convinced that God wanted her to expose Dr. Blackstone and the creeps who covered up the death of Todd Rice and sold the lethal drugs to Kat. But the way things were going, she was powerless to get away from people who probably wanted her dead, too.

In the silence, she heard a voice inside her head whisper, "My power is made perfect in weakness."

"Fine," she said aloud. "I believe you, Jesus—so, like, right now would be a perfect time for a miracle . . . maybe along the lines of parting the Red Sea. Unless, of course, while I surrender the photos to the Russians, you want me to give them Reverend Bud's phone with the secret message, too—"

Her heart leaped. *Why didn't I think of that before?* she wondered. She still had Reverend Bud's cell phone in her left pants pocket. The revelation lifted her spirits. *"Thank you, Jesus,"* she whispered. She smiled for the first time that she could remember that day.

Jodi carefully withdrew the phone and flipped it open. She noticed it was a sophisticated, high-end model with more features than the one she used. Same basic principle. His, however, had a color display and Web access—not that she'd be instant-messaging anybody anytime soon.

Jodi turned left onto Cottman Avenue and headed northwest. The Suburban did the same. She'd reach Roosevelt Boulevard in seven blocks and hoped to lose her tail in the four lanes of traffic. She dialed the number for information.

A robotic, mechanical-sounding voice asked: "What listing?"

"Phil Meyer." Jodi spoke his name with deliberate diction, hoping the computer voice system Bell Atlantic used would recognize the name.

"What city?"

"Huntingdon Valley," she said.

The machine provided the number and then added: "I can connect you for a charge of ninety-five cents. Press the pound key to accept this option."

She pressed pound, and then whispered a prayer he'd be home.

"Connecting," Mr. Computer Voice said.

"Hello? It's Rosie . . ."

"Hey, Mrs. Meyer—," Jodi started to say, but was forced to stop.

"We're not available right now. Kindly leave a message at the beep and one of us will get back to you. Have a pleasant day!"

Jodi was on the verge of tears again. She was so close, yet so far. The tone blasted in her ear. She started to speak, but her throat was dry. She cleared her throat. "Um, Phil, it's Jodi Adams. I really, *really* needed to talk with you right now. Gosh, I wish you were there. I just don't know what to do! See, like . . . where do I even start—"

"Try the beginning," she heard Phil say.

"Tell me I'm dreaming!" Jodi was elated.

"Sorry about that," he said. "I was outside grilling steaks. Didn't hear the phone ring. What's up? You okay?"

"Things aren't good, Phil. I . . . I'm so scared—"

"Take a deep breath, Jodi."

She did.

"Now, take it slow." She could tell Phil was listening intently. She had never met a man so focused and so clearheaded in a crisis. It felt reassuring to hear his voice.

"Okay. See, I've got a guy tailing me at this very second. My car is almost out of gas. I know some things, like, about a dead boy who's missing. He's Todd Rice. It's all kinda connected to the Pet Vet Wellness Center."

"I know the place." Phil's voice remained calm.

"Um, well, that's where his body is, oh, and I've got photos to prove everything. Plus, Kat's in the hospital—"

"Jodi, I want you to do exactly what I tell you."

"But what if—"

"Shut up and listen," Phil said, his tone was firm, not hostile. "You're gonna make it, Jodi. You can do this. Just like how you handled the houseboat situation, right?"

Somehow the thought of what she'd gone through two months ago wasn't real comforting at the moment. "Um, sure . . . right. So you believe me, then?"

"You, Jodi, of all people, wouldn't lie. Where are you now?" Phil asked.

"I think a few blocks away from Route 1." She stole another look behind her.

"Roosevelt Boulevard. Good. You're probably fifteen minutes away. Now, turn on your high beams."

Jodi did as instructed. "Okay, now what?"

"I want you to drive as quickly and as safely as possible to the parking lot across the street from the Pet Vet. Do you know the one?"

"I think so, the . . . uh, where that flower shop is, right?"

"Exactly. Don't stop for any reason until you get there."

"Well, I hadn't planned on any shopping," she said with a nervous laugh. "What about red lights?"

"Run 'em!"

"What?" Jodi pressed the phone against her ear. "I thought you said to run them?" Jodi wasn't liking the sound of this.

"I did. Of course, slow down. Do it safely. Tap your horn as you go. I just don't want you to be a sitting target. Got it?"

"I hear you." She glanced in her mirror. "Um, Phil, the Suburban is, like, two cars back."

"Just keep moving. When you get to Roosevelt, take the center three lanes. There'll be less of a chance for a delay. Stay focused and get to that flower shop. I'll contact Lieutenant Jim Johnson," Phil said. "I'll tell him what you've told me. He'll be waiting in that spot with several officers. Pull your car up next to them and wait until he says you can come out."

"But, Phil, the police have been, like, paid off. Reverend Bud said so himself—" Jodi felt the sweat dampening her forehead.

"Not this man. I'd bet my life on it," Phil said with conviction. "He's an ex-Seal. Different platoon. But we've worked together. I've known him for years. You'll be in good hands. And, I'll get there as soon as I can, okay?"

"That'd be awesome!"

"With a little luck," Phil said, "you won't run out of gas."

Luck? It'd be a miracle, Jodi thought.

This had better be good," Dr. Blackstone said, dressed in green scrubs, his cell phone flattened against his ear. He stood five feet away from the operating table in the basement level of the Pet Vet Wellness Center. Disposable yellow-paper booties covered his three-hundred-dollar loafers. He'd had to dispose of his blood-soaked rubber gloves before answering.

"Say me this, Comrade," Illya said. "Why think blonde girl goes with longhaired friend?"

Dr. Blackstone scratched the back of his head. "I'm in the middle of a procedure," he said. "I've got three donors to do before tonight. I don't have time for your riddles. Try speaking English—"

Dr. Blackstone heard Illya spit. "Me thinks good doctor should careful with words be," Illya said.

"And I think you," Dr. Blackstone snapped back, "should get to the point of this interruption." He crossed his arms as he waited for a response, and his jaw ground his teeth. From the background noise in the cell phone, he assumed Illya and Zhenya were in traffic. "Where are you?"

After a prolonged pause, Illya said, "We follow blonde girl. Close now to Philmont Street."

Dr. Blackstone's jaw stopped grinding. His brow tensed.

Illya continued. "She thinks smart to hiding longhaired man in trunk. You know this girl?"

Dr. Blackstone pictured her face. "Jodi," he said with contempt. His eyes narrowed as the pieces of a puzzle refused to fit together.

When his secretary returned from the InstyFoto Mart empty-handed, she figured Reverend Bud must have taken the photos. Especially in light of the clerk's comment that a longhaired man already picked them up. But what interest would Reverend Bud have in them? Dr. Blackstone wasn't sure.

What was Reverend Bud up to?

The question had haunted Dr. Blackstone all afternoon. Maybe this had to do with his last conversation with Reverend Bud, who seemed dead serious about walking away from their arrangement. And, what was Jodi doing with Reverend Bud? If that little Crusader Rabbit do-gooder didn't get the hint to back off after the spider treatment, then Dr. Blackstone would see to it that she got the message this time.

"Say me what you want," Illya said.

"I want her out of the picture," Dr. Blackstone barked. "Do you understand me? Smash her car. Push her off the road." He waved his arms like a wild man as he spoke. "Then, bring the reverend to me, got it?"

"J-yes. How you say, swell idea? We kill two birds with one rock," Illya said with a wicked chuckle.

Dr. Blackstone gritted his teeth. "You mean, with one *stone*."

✳ ✳ ✳

It was the *not knowing* that created the most anxiety for Jodi. At the moment, she had been driven crazy not knowing why the ugly, testosterone-charged black beast still followed her every move. Never too close, and never too far. While it wasn't exactly a high-speed car chase, the truck stuck to her like a bad cold.

She'd turn. They'd turn.

She'd slow. They'd slow.

She'd run a light. They'd do the same.

After the first time she ran a red light and they followed, it erased any question in her mind that they were on her tail.

But why? What did they want with her? And what were they waiting for? What kind of cat-and-mouse game was this?

Oddly, her cat, Houdini, came to mind. Houdini, she recalled, liked to trap a mouse and then play with it for an hour before going in for the final kill. *Was that the deal?* she wondered.

Jodi checked her watch. Based on the time, and on the fact that she had just turned onto Philmont Avenue, she figured she was less than five or six minutes from the parking lot where she hoped Phil and a hundred storm troopers were waiting.

Her heart leaped.

The end really was in sight.

For an instant, she considered listening to the message Reverend Bud had recorded. She'd want to provide the police with all the details. Just as quickly as the idea popped into her mind, she dismissed it. She was all thumbs when it came to electronic gadgets. *I'd probably erase it*, she thought.

It had been a long minute since Jodi last checked her mirror.

She glanced back and gasped.

The Suburban's massive, black steel winch, like a can opener, was poised to rip the lid off her trunk. She gritted her teeth and braced for the impact. Her right foot jammed the accelerator into the floor mat as far as it would go.

Jodi thought she heard the Suburban snort like an angry bull. The first hit knocked the wind out of her. Her shoulder harness strained against the force of her body, almost displacing her left shoulder. Her head snapped back against the headrest.

"Oh, Jesus!"

She wrestled with the steering wheel, trying to keep from careening off the narrow, two-lane road. She overcompensated in the process. The Mazda swerved left across the double yellow line— then right—then left again as she struggled to regain control; the tires burned their fingerprints into the pavement.

"Oh, my Jesus . . . help!"

She managed to straighten out the car and then stole a look in her rearview mirror. The truck was gone. At the same time that she realized she was no longer being followed, she felt the sunlight on her left disappear.

Jodi snapped her head around. Blackness filled her view. The Suburban's four-inch, side-mounted exhaust pipes snarled like a rabid dog at her side. She couldn't believe they were driving in the lane reserved for oncoming traffic.

Those guys are crazy, she thought. *We're all gonna die!*

The oversize tires from the SUV clutched the asphalt road with such intensity, Jodi could hear the pavement roar in protest. The Russians swerved to sideswipe her car. Jodi, hands drenched with sweat, yanked the wheel to avoid contact.

The Russians swerved again, this time taking a larger bite out of the space between them. The sick sound of metal against metal filled the air. Jodi was knocked sharply to her right from the impact on the left. A knifelike blast of pain pierced her side as her seat belt dug into her rib cage.

Jodi's Mazda 626, no longer able to maintain its spot, straddled the road and the unpaved shoulder three inches below it. Gravel kicked up against the bottom of her car. Dust billowed out from underneath, leaving a cloud of dirt in her wake.

Jodi's tears rolled down her face, mixing with her perspiration. "I can't hold on, Jesus," she said. "Help me!" It was then that she noticed a small circus of red-and-blue lights whirling in the distance. *Police!* Jodi thought.

She felt a rush of joy at the sight.

They were the length of a couple of football fields away.

The Russians must have seen them, too, she guessed when the Suburban suddenly dropped back in line behind her. She was going to let them have a piece of her mind once they were surrounded by the police. "And I'll have Bruce, like, do the bodywork on my car," she said aloud with a tear-stained smile.

Her smile quickly faded. *They're gonna slam me again!*

The instant she finished her thought, the Suburban plowed into the back left end of her car. They pushed her off the road toward an embankment of tall trees.

Jodi leaped on the brakes with both feet. She had been doing fifty on the road. The brakes shuddered and quaked as the antilock feature kicked in. Rock fragments, pebbles, and pieces of trash flew in every direction.

Three seconds later, she felt the rear end of the car lift in the air as the jaws from the Suburban worked against her braking effort. Instinctively, Jodi released the brakes, pounced on the gas, and turned away from the tree line.

The maneuver almost worked.

She braced herself as her right front bumper clipped an oak tree. The impact didn't stop her forward motion. She wasn't prepared for the simultaneous blast from the Mazda's passive restraint system. The light brown air bag detonated on impact and, with a blast, prevented her face from hitting the dash.

It deflated almost as fast as it had deployed. Only now, the air bag draped over the steering wheel, making her driving all but impossible. She was driving on nothing more than pure adrenaline.

She managed to get half of the car back onto the road. With a yank of the wheel, she swerved the other end into place. As she did, her right front tire hit a pothole. With a thunk, Jodi felt the rim of the wheel bash against the jagged edge of the gaping cavity.

Jodi felt the car lean to the right, hobbled by a flat tire. She wasn't about to let that prevent her from reaching the oasis of help, now fifty yards ahead. She had to straighten her rearview mirror before she could see what was going on behind her. She looked and, to her amazement, all she could make out was the back door of the Suburban disappearing in the opposite direction.

Thankful she was out of danger and, with the parking lot in view, Jodi stepped on the brakes.

Her heart almost burst when nothing happened.

She mashed the brake pedal repeatedly. Still nothing.

Jodi looked up. She was heading directly for the side of the flower shop building.

"Dear Jesus!"

She reached for the parking brake between the seats and pulled up with all her might. The rear brakes locked, sending the car into a half-spin. It slid forty feet until the right side of the car slammed into the wall of the flower shop.

On impact, Jodi banged her head against the window on her left. She blacked out.

Jodi's eyes opened with a series of repeated blinks. She was alive, that much registered. But she couldn't find answers fast enough for the deluge of questions flooding her mind. What had happened? Why was her air bag draped across the steering wheel and into her lap? Why did everything hurt so much?

Slowly, everything came back into focus.

Reverend Bud. The Russians. The car chase. The crash.

Jodi tried to wiggle her toes. They worked. She attempted to move her hands and found them to be numb, yet functioning. When she struggled to sit upright, her body yelled at her. Her muscles felt as stiff as they had after the first day of hockey camp.

She didn't know how long she'd been sitting behind the wheel, but she figured it couldn't have been too long. Several police officers were just steps away from reaching her door.

The cavalry had arrived.

She inhaled a full breath of air. "Ouch!" A sharp pain in her right side warned her to go easy.

"Are you all right, miss?" The first policeman to reach the car carefully opened her door.

Jodi offered a weak smile. "Um, so far, so good, I think."

A taller, older man, in his midforties she guessed, came alongside the first cop. "You must be Jodi Adams." His eyes had a soft warmth to them, although his face appeared to be rough like weathered rawhide. "I'm Lieutenant Jim Johnson, Phil Meyer's friend."

"Is he here?" Jodi asked, her eyes scanning the parking lot.

"He's on the way," Lieutenant Johnson said. "Listen, I know you want to get out of there. But I'd suggest you sit tight. The paramedics will make sure everything checks out before you move. How do you feel?"

"Like a crash-test dummy." She smiled. What she wanted most was a hot soak in the tub for about three weeks. "My right side hurts some when I breathe."

"Understood. Jodi, you are one remarkable girl," Lieutenant Johnson said. "You have no idea how many lives you've saved today with your tip." His sport coat hung open as he stood beside the car. His left arm rested on the roof to shade her from the sun. She observed the end of his gun in his shoulder holster.

"How's that?" Jodi said.

"You've helped us bust Blackstone's operation," Lieutenant Johnson said. "I'm a detective on the force and we've been aware of his little enterprise for several months. Just didn't have the proof to bring him down."

Jodi nodded. "I can't believe a vet, of all people, would, like, mass-produce drugs and sell them to kids."

Lieutenant Johnson's eyebrow shot up at that piece of information. "Drugs? He was manufacturing drugs? We weren't aware of—"

"Excuse me, coming through," said the shorter of two paramedics who nudged their way past Lieutenant Johnson and his side officer. "Name's Bill. This is my assistant, Tom. Let's have a look here." Bill placed a medium-size first-aid kit on the ground, and then squatted by Jodi.

"I really feel okay," Jodi said. "My right side is kinda sore. Other than that I'm—"

"Did you black out at any time, ma'am?" Bill examined her eyes.

"Yeah, for like a second, I think."

"How many fingers am I holding up?" Bill said.

"Three. Really, I feel fine," Jodi said.

"Can you feel this?" He pricked her ankles with a pointy object.

"Yes." In the distance, Jodi caught a glimpse of the flurry of activity across the street at the Pet Vet clinic. Police and medics were crawling all over the place.

"Where did you say it was sore?" Bill asked.

"Right here." Jodi pointed to the right side of her rib cage.

Bill turned to Tom. "She may have a light concussion," Bill said. "Probably nothing serious. But we'll need to take her to Abington to have a look at that side. She might have a fractured rib." Tom turned and headed for the ambulance.

"Hold on. I've got to talk to her right now," Lieutenant Johnson said. "Got to have her identify a body. Then she's all yours. Just give me five minutes to wrap this up, okay?"

The medic nodded. "Five minutes it is." Bill unbuckled her seat belt and then helped her out of the car. Tom returned with a gurney a minute later. Bill and Tom lifted her onto a stretcher, placing her head into a brace. They strapped her in place and then secured the stretcher on the gurney, which, with its wheeled legs, was elevated about four feet above ground.

Lieutenant Johnson came to her side. "Jodi, you mentioned something about Dr. Blackstone's involvement with drugs. What more can you tell me?"

Jodi wasn't sure where to begin. So much had happened so quickly. "Well . . . Dr. Blackstone would, like, fill syringes with ketamine," Jodi said. "Actually, the people who worked for him did that part. Anyway, his partner, Reverend Bud, would sell the stuff at these, um, dance parties that they sponsored." Jodi paused when the paramedic appeared at her side.

"Excuse the interruption," Bill said to Lieutenant Johnson. "I'd like to get an IV in her."

Jodi closed her eyes and gritted her teeth as he stuck her arm with the needle. When he was finished, she said, "I only found out about all this because my friend Kat and this guy Todd Rice got some at a party last night. She's in the hospital and Todd died. I figured Dr. Blackstone's, like, trying to cover up Todd's death, so he took the body. Isn't that what this is all about?"

"Actually, no," Lieutenant Johnson said. He hesitated. He appeared to be deep in thought.

"Well, then, what's up?" Jodi asked. "I thought you said you've been tracking his business or whatever for months."

Lieutenant Johnson leaned his head to one side. "I guess since this will hit the papers in a day or so, I'll fill you in." He placed his arm on his hip. "Blackstone devised what I'm sure he considered to be the brilliant scheme of providing the black market with vital organs—human organs."

He let that sink in.

Jodi gasped. "You mean . . . body parts? . . . but why? How?"

"There's a world shortage of hearts, livers, kidneys, corneas—even genitals," Lieutenant Johnson began. "If you needed a liver or a heart, you'd have to place a request with the government-contracted United Network for Organ Sharing agency and then wait. Sometimes for months or years. They're the only authorized outlet for organs in the U.S."

"Gee, I had no idea Dr. Blackstone was, like, into all that," Jodi said, still stunned at the revelation of his secret activity. "I knew the guy was a creep!"

Lieutenant Johnson nodded. "People with big bucks are willing to pay anything, especially if their lives depend on it. A single heart brings upward of $60,000, a liver $40,000, a kidney $3,000 to $8,000. The money was too juicy for Blackstone to pass up."

"But isn't that illegal?"

"Absolutely." Lieutenant Johnson nodded. "Harvesting human organs *is* illegal, not to mention unethical. But it's done in other countries, like China, for example. From what we can tell, Dr. Blackstone saw himself as a pioneer—as a modern-day Robin Hood. He took from the poor and gave to the needy highest bidder."

"That's so sick." Jodi would have shook her head, but the brace held fast. "So, what's all this got to do with the rave parties?"

"Simple," Lieutenant Johnson said. "See, his raves provided the perfect cover. They were hosted in unregulated sites."

Jodi's mind drifted back to what she'd seen the night before. She wondered what would have happened if she and Bruce hadn't taken Kat out of there. Would Kat have become one of Dr. Blackstone's donors? And what if the Russians had caught *her*, Jodi wondered. Her stomach gurgled.

Lieutenant Johnson turned his head and looked across the street. He looked back at Jodi. "By the time the authorities were requested to investigate a missing person at a rave, such as this Todd Rice you alerted us to, the raves would be, like the circus, gone. The chance of tracing a victim's disappearance was nil."

"I . . . I can't believe this!" Jodi felt dizzy. "So, like, they made money selling tickets to the rave, plus the drugs. But the real cash was in—" She couldn't bring herself to say the words. "Um, no wonder when I went back with the police, Todd's body was already gone. But where did they hide his body?"

"In a Ryder truck," Lieutenant Johnson said. "We got a lucky break about a month ago from an auto repair shop employee who serviced the truck. While working on the tailgate, he opened the rear door and noticed the back of the truck was crudely outfitted with a mini surgical suite—"

Jodi interrupted him. "Hey, I saw a truck just like that outside of Reverend Bud's today."

"If you give me the address, I'll get a man right over there," Lieutenant Johnson said. "See, we figured this Reverend Bud character would place the bodies in back and hook them up to individual ventilators to keep the blood circulating to their organs. We've been watching the clinic and noticed this truck coming at all hours of the night, but we didn't have enough for a search warrant—that is, until now. Your tip provided the probable cause.

We've got our men crawling all over Blackstone this very minute."

Jodi lit up. "Oh, I've got something else for you. In my car. There's a cell phone that belongs to Reverend Bud. He told me he wanted, like, out of all this. Now I can see why. Anyway, he recorded a conversation with Dr. Blackstone that might help."

"Excellent," Lieutenant Johnson said. "As best we can tell, the truck would arrive at Blackstone's clinic where the 'donors' would be transported to a full surgical suite in the clinic's basement. He'd remove and place on ice the vital parts for immediate red-label shipment. Again, thanks to you, you could say we caught him red-handed."

"That is so whacked." Jodi swallowed hard.

"What we haven't figured out," Lieutenant Johnson said, "is how Blackstone distributed the organs abroad."

Jodi bit her lip. "Okay, I can't prove this, but I'd say the Russians must have had something to do with it."

"Russians?"

"Reverend Bud said something about a couple of Russians," Jodi offered. "I think they're the same guys who, like, ran me over."

Lieutenant Johnson's radio crackled. "Yes?"

"We're ready for the identification, sir," the voice said.

*　*　*

With the aid of the paramedics, Jodi was transported to the loading dock area of the Pet Vet. As she waited to identify the body, she heard a scuffle coming from within the double door. She recognized the voice. It was a voice she wouldn't soon forget. A moment later, she saw Dr. Blackstone, handcuffed, walking between two officers who gripped his arms.

Jodi locked eyes with him. Dr. Blackstone looked like a crazed animal. "Wasn't it you who said, 'The game of life has rules'?" Jodi said as he passed. "Well, I'd say it's game over . . . *pal.*"

"You making fun of me, girl?" Dr. Blackstone's upper lip was curled into a snarl. "This *isn't* over, Jodi Adams." He lunged in her direction and spit on the ground. The officers jerked Dr. Blackstone back toward the direction of the squad car.

Jodi's heart pounded the inside of her chest with the intensity of a jackhammer. She could feel the raw evil radiating around him. How could somebody become so possessed by such vicious inhumanity?

A minute later, Jodi watched as an officer, accompanied by Lieutenant Johnson, wheeled a body in a black body bag out the back door. Lieutenant Johnson unzipped the bag about eighteen inches. He circled around the gurney and elevated Jodi for a clear view. He said, "Jodi, is this the boy you saw? Todd Rice?"

Jodi bit her bottom lip and then looked.

Her eyes welled up with hot tears.

"*Dear Jesus . . . ,*" Jodi said, her voice breaking. "Oh my, gosh . . . I—I can't believe it. No, sir. That's Carlos . . . Carlos Martinez . . . He was . . . a friend from school."

odi stood in the hall just outside Kat's hospital room. She held an arrangement of flowers in one hand, her pocket New Testament in the other. She hesitated. Jodi stared at the placard on the door—Room 210—and took a deep breath.

Jodi longed for Kat to give her life to Christ and prayed this would be a divine appointment. All day yesterday she had prayed for the right words to say. She had even rehearsed them a hundred times in her head.

Jodi wanted to find a graceful way to help Kat see that she was designed for heaven. Jodi believed that Kat, rather than embrace the gift of eternal life, had always settled for an illusion: the music, the drugs, the altered state of mind. Even the PLUR goal was artificial when compared to what Jesus offered.

Jodi whispered a quick prayer and then tapped lightly on the door. In some ways, she felt more nervous now than when she entered a school debate situation, because the outcome of this time with Kat was eternally more important.

"Come in," Kat said.

Jodi opened the door. Kat was sitting upright with a food tray positioned across her lap. The oxygen line was still taped in place under Kat's nose. Two IV bags now fed the tube running down her arm and into her vein. Her eyes were shadowed by dark circles and her skin was, like her sheets, a pale white.

"Hey, girlfriend!" Kat said with a wide smile. "You're just in time for lunch. Let's see," Kat said, lifting a round, three-inch stainless-steel cover from the plate in front of her. "Um, we've got red and green Jell-O cubes. Want some?" Kat took a bite.

Jodi relaxed a little at the warm greeting. She smiled and walked to the end of the bed. "I think I'll pass."

"Smart woman," Kat said. She put down the spoon. "What's with the shiner? You okay?"

"Oh, that. Yeah. It's a long story," Jodi said. Her side still ached from a fractured rib. Jodi's doctor had informed her the best way to treat her rib was to leave it alone. "How about you? You're looking better."

Kat shrugged. "Guess so."

"Hey, I brought these for you," Jodi said, and then placed the flowers on the bedstand.

"Flowers? For me? How sweet!" Kat admired the arrangement. "Listen, there's something I wanted to talk about—"

"Actually, me first. I owe you an apology." Jodi took a seat by Kat's bed and then fidgeted with a ring on her finger.

"For what?" Kat took a sip from her juice cup.

"I misjudged you, Kat." Jodi looked up. "All this time I was so mad at you . . . see, I thought you had, like, taken those drugs at the rave. I couldn't believe you'd betray me like that, you know?"

"What makes you think I didn't?" Kat leaned her head back against the pillow.

"Your doctor told me a minute ago," Jodi pulled her hair back. "He said your blood work didn't show any signs of drugs. So, give me details. What happened? I mean, I found the syringe, like, right next to you."

Kat nodded. "I know. Talk about crazy. I was dancing with that guy—"

"Todd Rice."

"Uh-huh. Well, we went upstairs to chill," Kat said. "Next thing I knew, he was shooting up. I tried to talk him out of it, even yanked a needle away from him, but I was too late."

Jodi thought about that for a moment. "You mean, he used *both* needles?"

Kat nodded. "Funny thing is, before I met you that would've been me."

"Then why was your body, like, freaking out?" Jodi asked.

"Doctor says I started to reject your kidney," Kat said. "Nothing personal, mind you."

They both laughed.

"What a coincidence, huh?" Kat said. "But thanks to you, I got here in time. Got me some super-duper antirejection drugs."

"So will you forgive me?" Jodi hooked her hair behind her ears.

"Of course I will," Kat said with a smile. "But, Jodi, tell me this. Am I gonna, you know, make it?" Kat searched her eyes.

"Hey, what kind of question is that?"

"Come on, level with me," Kat said. "I'm a big girl."

Jodi wasn't sure it was her place to say. On the other hand, Jodi realized she was, in some ways, the only family Kat had right now. Kat's heart monitor ticked away in the silence.

"Well, the doctor seems to think your chances are, like, better than fifty-fifty," Jodi said. "And I'm praying for you every day." Jodi reached forward and gave Kat a reassuring pat.

Kat folded her hands. "Well, that's what I wanted to talk about. See, I've been thinking . . . about stuff. I've really got to get, like, a handle on my life, you know? And I think you know the way."

"You mean—" Jodi wasn't expecting this.

Kat nodded. "I want what you have."

Jodi's heart jumped so hard, she wondered if Kat had heard it pound. "Well . . . it's like we talked about before . . . at Young Life, you know? That Jesus gave his life so we'd have true peace . . . that our sin keeps us from God and, um, when we ask him into our hearts, he makes us brand-new."

"I know. I remember hearing that, but I guess I just don't get it," Kat said. Tears started to gently roll down her face. "Why me? Why would Jesus want to rescue a used-up druggie like me? I mean, what's in it for him?"

"Kat, listen to me," Jodi said, fighting back tears of her own. "Jesus said that a doctor comes to heal those who are sick—not those who have it all together. Jesus loves us so much that he died for *all* of us."

"Yeah, maybe for someone like you, but how can you be so sure he loves *me*?" Kat searched Jodi's eyes.

Jodi didn't need to open her Bible. Instead, she closed her eyes and softly repeated the words she knew so well. "'For God so loved the world that he gave his one and only Son, that whoever believes in him shall not perish but have eternal life.'"

When Jodi opened her eyes, Kat reached over and extended her hand to Jodi. "Help me pray . . . would you?"

"In a heartbeat!" Jodi took her hand and leaned forward. "Maybe you could just repeat this prayer in your heart, okay?"

Kat nodded.

Before Jodi had a chance to pray, she heard the door behind her burst open.

"What did I miss?" Bruce said, sweeping into the room without knocking.

Jodi and Kat looked over at him.

"It's a God thing, Bruce," Jodi said, her eyes moistened by fresh tears. "Kat wants to pray. Care to join us?"

"Um, hey, why don't I take a rain check," Bruce said as he took a step backwards. "If you don't mind, I'll just wait over here in this chair until you guys are done."

"Sure thing," Jodi said. She turned back to Kat and, with a wink, said, "You ready?"

"Go for it," Kat said.

Jodi cleared her throat. "Dear Jesus," she began, remembering the prayer she prayed years ago. "I need you . . . I know my sin keeps me from you . . . but you died on the cross in my place. I want to live for you, now. I believe you are the way, the truth, and the life. Please come into my life today. In Jesus' name, amen."

"Amen," Kat said.

Jodi opened her eyes and saw a smile filling Kat's face. Jodi leaned over the bed to embrace Kat. They laughed and cried for a long minute.

"Ahem," Bruce said. "I hate to break up the lovefest, but I've got some major news."

Jodi released Kat turned toward Bruce. "You know," she said as she wiped away her tears with the back of her hand, "sometimes you can be about as sensitive as sand paper."

Bruce shrugged off the friendly jab. He stood up and started to walk toward Kat's bedside. "Whoa! That's some shiner, Jodi," Bruce said as he approached. "Let me guess. You got into a fight with your parents over trashing their car, right?"

"Hardly."

Bruce grabbed the newspaper he was carrying under his arm. "Hey, did you see this story? Right on the front page. Check it out, Jodi. Looks like you've got your first really big scoop!" He unfolded the paper and held it out for them to see.

"What story? What scoop?" Kat said, drying her tears, too.

"How much time do you have?" Jodi said with a laugh.

"Oh, and Jodi, I just heard from Phil. He said there's a good chance Reverend Bud is gonna make it, thanks to your 911 call," Bruce said.

"Really? That's so cool."

"Reverend who?" Kat asked.

"Don't worry, I'll fill you in later," Jodi said. "What about the Russians? Did they find them?"

The expression on Bruce's face turned suddenly serious. "Oh, I don't think so. But did you know that the police *released* Dr. Blackstone this morning?" He handed the paper to Jodi as he spoke. "And he said something about getting revenge."

Jodi felt the blood rush to her face.

His mouth morphed into a cheesy grin. "I'm just kidding . . ."

"*Bruce!*" Jodi said. She punched him in the arm.

"Feel free to hit him once for me, too!" Kat said.

Jodi loved to see the sparkle in Kat's eyes.

Also Available from Tim LaHaye

EIGHT TEENS VOLUNTEER FOR A REAL LIFE DIVERSITY EXPERIMENT AND END UP IN A BATTLE FOR SURVIVAL

TIM LAHAYE
AND BOB DEMOSS

EIGHT TEENS VOLUNTEER FOR A REAL LIFE DIVERSITY EXPERIMENT
AND END UP IN A BATTLE FOR SURVIVAL

A NOVEL

THE MIND SIEGE PROJECT

In the tradition of MTV's *The Real World*, eight high school juniors volunteer for a week on a houseboat in the name of experimental education. Rosie Meyer, the former Olympic silver medallist turned social studies teacher, dreams of her students learning first-hand the realities of tolerance and diversity. And learn they do. Although the students sail for a single week, the issues faced, the truths uncovered, and the lessons learned leave them changed for a lifetime.

W PUBLISHING GROUP
www.wpublishinggroup.com